Heartless

Connect With Me

EMAIL >> ervinkeisha@yahoo.com

TWITTER >> www.twitter.com/keishaervin

FACEBOOK >> www.facebook.com/keisha.ervin

INSTAGRAM >> @keishaervin

SNAPCHAT >> kyrese99

YOUTUBE >> www.youtube.com/ColorMePynk

Prologue

Chyna slowly made her way up the steps. A huge knot was in the pit of her stomach. She was sure that she and Tyreik were about to have a showdown. When she hit her bedroom she expected to be met with a barrage of questions. Instead, she was greeted with a piercing silence. The bedroom was completely empty. Tyreik was nowhere to be found.

The only trace of him ever being there was the lingering smell of his cologne in the air, the unmade bed and a gigantic scuff mark on the wall. Chyna examined the mark closer. She quickly came to the conclusion that Tyreik had thrown his phone at the wall in a fit of rage.

"He really needs to grow up." She shook her head and threw down her bag and phone.

Irritated by his childish behavior and the fact that he left the bed looking a mess, Chyna threw the covers back. She couldn't function if her bed was unmade. To her surprise, as she straightened the sheets, she found Tyreik's cellphone. Stunned that he would've been careless enough to leave it behind, she slowly picked it up.

Merely touching his phone was an unwritten rule that she was breaking. She hardly ever went near the thing in fear of Tyreik's wrath. He would bite her head off if he walked in and caught her holding it. Chyna stared at the phone. Cupping it in the palm of her hand was like winning the gold medal at the Olympics. There was no way she could resist not going through it.

She might not get another chance. Now was the perfect time. It was just her luck that his phone wasn't locked. Tyreik must've taken the lock off since she didn't come home. Chyna didn't hesitate to go into his text messages first. In it she found nothing but texts from her, his pot'nahs and business associates. If he did have a chick texting him, he'd already gotten rid of the evidence.

Next, she went through his pictures. There was hardly anything there except a few naked pics of her and screenshots of sneakers he wanted. The last thing she checked was his contacts. There were a few numbers saved under initials or single letters which she found odd.

She automatically assumed they were chicks he fucked with numbers.

Chyna could feel her blood pressure rise as she scrolled through the numbers. Then her heart all but stopped beating when she came across Rema's name. Tyreik swore that the thing between him and Rema was over. Why was her number in his phone again?

Chyna's palms began to sweat as a million thoughts swarmed her mind. What if they had started back fuckin' around? Had he been seeing her this whole time? Chyna couldn't bare the thought of going through the pain of him cheating on her again.

Before she could gather her thoughts, the familiar sound of Tyreik taking the steps two at a time pierced her ears. He must've realized he'd left his phone and came rushing back home. Chyna turned her head towards the stairs with tears in her eyes. She didn't even try to pretend like she wasn't going through his phone.

No, she was going to confront his lying, cheating-ass. Chyna stood looking like a wounded deer as Tyreik made it to the top of the steps. He eyed her with a stern expression on his face. He was still pissed that she hadn't come home the night before. He became even angrier when he spotted his phone in her hand.

"What you doing wit' my phone?"

"What it look like I was doing? I was going through it." Chyna quickly wiped her tears and regained her strength.

She refused to look weak in front of him. He'd broken her down one too many times.

"What I tell you about touching my shit?" He charged towards her and snatched his phone out of her hand. "This ain't yo' phone! You don't pay the bill on this muthafucka so don't touch it!" He pointed it in her face.

"I don't give a fuck about none of that! As long as you in this muthafucka I'ma touch whatever the fuck I want!"

"There you go threatening somebody 'cause yo' name on the lease. Get the fuck outta here wit' that! I got my own place, remember?"

"Mom! Can y'all stop fighting? I can hear y'all all the way downstairs!" India asked from the bottom of the staircase.

"India, go sit down!" Chyna yelled, feeling herself unraveling.

She knew she shouldn't have been arguing around her daughter but somehow it had become the norm for them. India rolled her eyes and did as she was told. She was so tired of her mother promising that things between her and Tyreik would get better. They would be at peace with one another only to be back at each others' throats days later. Their dysfunctional relationship was starting to wear on India. She only tolerated Tyreik for her mother's sake. She didn't hate him, because at times he could be nice, but most of the time he was an asshole.

"I'm finna go." Tyreik turned to leave.

"You ain't going nowhere!" Chyna pulled him back towards her. "Why the fuck you got that bitch number in yo' phone?" She gripped his arm tight.

"What bitch?" Tyreik eyed her confused.

"Don't play stupid. The bitch you cheated on me with."

"I ain't even tryin' to be funny but which bitch are you talkin' about?" Tyreik chuckled.

Chyna felt her heart sink. This nigga didn't give a fuck how he treated her. But how could she get mad at him? She'd allowed him to treat her like shit for years.

"Oh, so you think that shit is funny? I'm not laughing, Tyreik." She pushed his arm away.

"Yo, you buggin'. I ain't got time for this shit. You gon' make me late for my haircut." He tried to leave once more, only for Chyna to jump in his path.

"Fuck yo' haircut. What you tryin' to get fly for Rema or that wavy hair bitch? You tryin' to look cute to impress they bummy-ass? I saw her name in your phone, Tyreik. Why after over ten years is this bitch name still poppin' up? You still fuckin' her, aren't you?" Chyna questioned feeling herself become sick.

"You're fuckin' insane." Tyreik eyed her in disbelief. "First you snap on me at the bar, then you don't come home, then you go through my phone on some ole Inspector Gadget shit and now you accuse me of cheating just 'cause you saw a bitch number in my phone? You're fuckin' crazy."

"If I'm crazy it's because you made me this way. I'm tired of dealing wit' you and yo' shit! Every other second it's something different wit' you. I can't ever get a moment to breathe without the rug being pulled from underneath me!"

"Ain't nobody cheating on you!" Tyreik barked.

"Then why is her number in your phone? You still haven't answered the question." Chyna cocked her head to the side.

"And I'm not 'cause I ain't did nothin'. Did you go through my call log? Do you see me calling her? Do you see her callin' me? Do you see us textin' each other? No! 'Cause ain't shit going on. Just the bullshit you conjuring up in yo' head!" He pointed his finger in her face like a gun.

"I'm tired of you accusing me of shit I ain't do. Now I'm done talkin'. I'm about to go get my haircut." He pushed her out the way and jogged down the steps.

"Uh ah, Tyreik! Come back! I'm not done talkin' to you!" Chyna raced behind him.

She would be damned if he thought he was getting away that easy. He had some serious explaining to do. The answers he'd given her just weren't good enough.

"Tyreik, I'm not playin' wit you!" She yelled.

"Do it look like I'm laughing?" He said over his shoulder as he continued to walk. "You wanna be on that bullshit, be on it by yo'self. You're not about to ruin my day."

"Ruin your day?" Chyna repeated barely able to breathe.

Tyreik loved switching things around and making her feel like she was the problem.

"Nigga, how about you ruined my life!" Chyna mushed him in the back of his head as he made it to the front door.

"Mom, stop!" India pleaded jumping in front of her mother so she wouldn't hit Tyreik again. "Just let him go!"

Sorrow filled India's eyes. Her mom deserved so much more. She just didn't understand why she couldn't see it for herself. Tyreik spun around and charged towards her furiously.

"If I ruined your life, then why the fuck you still wit' me? Huh? If I'm such a horrible-ass person, then why you keep coming back? 'Cause you're full of shit, Chyna!" He mushed her in the forehead causing her head to jerk back. "You think life is one of them books you be writing. This ain't make-believe. This is real-life and if you put yo' hands on me again I'ma fuck you up!"

"Nigga, do you think that if I could write the perfect man for me that it would be you?" Chyna's bottom lip quivered. "You out yo' muthafuckin' mind! I'ma tell you what's real-life! What's real-life is you fuckin' that bitch! And when I find proof of it I'ma be done fuckin' wit' your ass for good!" Chyna leaped across India and popped Tyreik in the face.

"Don't put yo' hands on me no more, man!" Tyreik reached over India and grabbed Chyna by the arm.

His grip was so tight that she felt like she was losing the blood circulation in her arm.

"Tyreik, stop! Let her go!" India begged trying to push him off her mother.

"That's yo' ignorant-ass mama! Tell her to keep her fuckin' hands off of me! I told her to gone!" He threw her arm down angrily.

"Explain to me how you mad! I'm the one that caught you on some bullshit." Chyna tried to step past India to no avail.

Not wanting things to escalate any further, Tyreik opened the front door and slammed it shut behind him, almost causing the glass to shatter.

"Don't be slamming my goddamn door!" Chyna fumed. "Move, India!" She tried to push her out the way.

"Mom, chill. Just let him leave." India cornered her mother.

Chyna knew she should listen to her daughter. She was right but the rage inside of her veins had taken over. She couldn't see anything but red. She had to make him hurt. Tyreik had disrespected her for the last time. Not hearing her daughter, Chyna pushed her out of the way and raced out of the door. To her dismay, Tyreik had already made it to his car.

That didn't stop her from standing in front of his truck and slamming her fist into the hood. She didn't care that it was broad daylight or that her neighbors were outside. She needed him to see how much pain she was in. Tyreik however didn't care about her feelings. All he cared about was getting away from her stupid-ass before something crazy popped off.

He was so mad he was liable to slap the shit outta Chyna. The last thing he needed was the cops being called. Without paying attention to his surroundings, he placed the car in reverse and rammed his foot on the gas. The truck went flying backwards into the street. What Tyreik failed to realize was that a school bus was coming towards him.

Chyna's eyes widened with fear as the school bus crashed into the side of Tyreik's truck. The impact was so hard that the truck flipped over three times and landed on the roof. A blood curdling scream escaped from Chyna's lungs as she ran towards the driver's side. There Tyreik was dangling upside down with blood trickling from his forehead, nose and mouth. Broken glass was everywhere.

"India, call 911!" She screamed trying to open the door but the door was stuck.

India ran back in the house and did as she was told.

"Baby! Are you ok?" Chyna sobbed feeling like she was dying.

Tyreik couldn't even find the strength to respond. His heart rate was declining by the second. All he could do was take short, shallow breaths.

"Baby, answer me. Tell me you're ok. You have to be ok, Tyreik. I'm sorry. I'm so sorry." She wept caressing the side of his face.

Then the unthinkable happened. Tyreik's eyes started to flutter. It was taking every fiber of his being to keep his eyes open.

"No-no-no-no-no-no! You have to stay awake. Don't you fall asleep, Tyreik!" Chyna sobbed trying to keep him focused.

But Tyreik couldn't hold on any longer. His eyes were too heavy. With the little strength he had, he took one last look at Chyna then allowed his eyes to close.

"Noooooooo! Tyreik, wake up!" She patted his face repeatedly. "Wake up, please. Tyreik! I'm sorry! Wake up! Tyreik! WAAAAAAAAAAKE UP!!!!!!"

"Don't fuck around wit' no snake nigga." – Tia NoMore & Kehlani, "Or Nah"

#1

"Tyreik!" Chyna jumped up out of her sleep frantic.

Her heart was racing a mile a minute. She could barely catch her breath. She couldn't believe that this was happening to her again. She hadn't had a nightmare about Tyreik in months. During the day, she was able to get over the fact that he was no longer in her life but at night, memories of the day she lost him forever tormented her dreams.

No matter how hard she tried, she couldn't escape him. The ghost of him surrounded her wherever she went. It seeped inside her veins. It panged her heart knowing that the reason she'd lost him forever was all because of her unwillingness to leave well enough alone. Now here she was a year and a half later suffering from her mistake.

The world felt as if it were falling down around her. She had to regain control of herself and figure out where the hell she was at. The last thing she remembered was turning up in the club, getting white girl wasted and making out with some fine-ass Rotimi look-alike. Since losing Tyreik, having one-night stands had become the norm for Chyna. She refused to focus her attention on one man ever again. Her heart refused to suffer another lost.

Disoriented, she held her chest. For the life of her she couldn't figure out where she was. From the looks of things, she was in a hotel suite. Naked, she sat on top of a king-sized bed flanked by sliding doors. Across from the bedroom area was a living room with elegant furniture, sparkling chandeliers, a large work desk and modern amenities such as a flat screen TV, internet access and more. Chyna's head was spinning out of control. It wasn't until she heard a loud knock on the door that she realized her whereabouts.

"This is the Four Seasons hotel management! Open up!" A woman continued to knock profusely.

"What the hell?" Chyna mumbled, startled.

Annoyed with the loud banging, she looked to her left for the guy she'd slept with but dude was nowhere to be found.

"Just a minute!" She responded angrily.

"No! We need you to open the door now!" The female voice yelled.

"I said just a minute goddamit!" Chyna fumed.

She was desperately trying to figure out what all the commotion was about. *Where is this nigga at,* she thought. *Maybe he's in the bathroom.*

"Ma'am, this is the police! If you don't open this door right this second we're going to be forced to come in!" A male officer warned.

"Just a second! I'm naked!" Chyna panicked as the door was unlocked and pushed open.

Swiftly, she wrapped the sheets around her naked body and stood up.

"Are you fuckin' kidding me?" She asked still hung over and half asleep. "What in the hell is going on?"

"It's past checkout time and this room hasn't been paid for." The older, female, hotel manager said with an attitude. "If we don't receive payment we're going to be forced to press charges."

"Ma'am, we're going to need you to get dressed and take care of the payment because as of right now, you're illegally squatting." The officer urged.

"How could I be illegally squatting when we were given a room key?" She grabbed the key off the nightstand and held it up forcefully.

"We?" The officer looked around the suite with his hand on his gun.

"Calm down, Darren Wilson," Chyna mocked the white cop. "Nobody needs to get shot today. The guy I came with is in the bathroom." She unlocked the door only to find it empty.

Worried, she frantically searched the room for the guy she banged the night before. None of his belongings were there. He was gone.

"There's no one here but you, ma'am." The snooty manager said with an attitude. "Have you been drinking?

Are you on any kind of illegal substance?" She eyed her quizzically.

"First of all." Chyna held the covers up over her breasts. "Crack is wack. Am I still hung-over from last night? Yes. Now I came here last night with this dude. When we got the room the girl at the front desk said that the system was down and that he could give her his credit card info when we checked out. Now I don't know where ole boy is but I'm not paying for this damn room. I can tell you that right now."

"What is this man's name?" The officer asked taking out a pad and a pen.

Chyna stood and thought for a second but she couldn't remember his name for shit.

"I don't remember." She finally responded.

"So you mean to tell me you got a hotel room with a man and you don't even know his name?" The hotel manager shot with an attitude.

"Don't judge me, girl. You don't know my life." Chyna mean mugged her.

"Listen, ma'am, if you want to avoid jail time you're going to have to pay for this room." The officer stated.

"How much is the suite?" Chyna huffed, rolling her eyes.

"Two thousand dollars." The hotel manager smirked crossing her arms across her chest.

"Oh hell to the naw!" Chyna threw her hands up in the air forgetting all she wore was a sheet.

By the time she realized what she'd done, it was already too late. Her 36 DD breasts were on full display for the hotel manager and officer to see.

"Wow." The officer gulped unable to take his eyes off her voluptuous caramel breasts.

Utterly embarrassed, Chyna quickly lifted the sheet back over her titties.

"Let's just pretend that didn't happen." Her face burned red.

"Oh but it did." The hotel manager snarled unimpressed.

"Girl, bye. Don't hate," Chyna flicked her wrist. "You wish you still had titties like this." She opened the sheet and flashed her boobs.

"Officer, get this woman out of here." The hotel manager rolled her eyes. "She's obviously high off bath salts. I have a hotel to run. I don't have time for this. At this point, she's either going to pay the bill or go to jail. It's up to you, boo." The hotel manager looked Chyna up-and-down then turned her back to leave.

"Girl, you betta get yo' life." Chyna warned ready to pounce.

She didn't give a fuck that the woman was old. Her old-ass could get it.

"It ain't my fault you ain't got dicked down since 1872."

"Ma'am, please get dressed so we can resolve this situation. I'll be waiting outside the door." The officer assured, closing the door behind him.

Overwhelmed, confused and stressed the fuck out, Chyna plopped down onto the bed. It was apparently clear that the dude she'd smashed had dipped on her and stiffed her with the bill. She had the two grand for the bill but she didn't have the two grand to spend. Chyna was a single mother. She couldn't be out in the streets tricking off two grand like it was nothing.

Pissed wasn't even the word to describe how she felt. But she couldn't be mad at anyone but herself. She should've got up and left after realizing the dick was a dud. The nigga was fine as fuck but his stroke game was offensive to her soul. He was heavy as hell on top of her. It felt like a boulder was lying on her chest. He was fucking her like he had just won the porn star of the year award but in reality, Chyna, nor her pussy felt a thing.

Chyna didn't need this type of added stress in her life. It was already freaking her out that she had another nightmare about Tyreik. On top of that, her fifteen-year-old daughter, India, was abroad for the summer backpacking through Europe with her school. She'd only been gone a week but for Chyna it already felt like an eternity. Being by herself for three months would give Chyna the much needed time she needed to figure out her life. She was barely hanging on by a thread and bullshit like this was only making matters worse.

"Fuck my life." She lie back on the bed and stared at the ceiling. "I need a drink ASAP."

"Can't go home alone again.

Need someone to numb the pain." –

Tove Lo, "Habits (Stay High)"

#2

Five o'clock that afternoon, Chyna sat on the edge of her bed in one of Tyreik's old wife-beaters and a pair of panties. His old, platinum chain with a Jesus piece hung from her neck. Weed smoke passed through her lips as she listened to Wale's *Bad*. After the morning she had, getting high was the only way she was going to relax. A million thoughts ran through her clouded mind. Instead of getting high, she should've been working on her book.

Chyna was an extremely successful author. She'd been in the game for eleven years and had written twenty-one stories. She was regarded in the literary game as one of the best. In the beginning of her career she thoroughly enjoyed writing but over the last few years, especially after losing Tyreik, she lost interest in the craft.

The pressure to remain on top, outdo herself and please her audience was becoming increasingly difficult. Some of her audience wanted her to go back to writing more street orientated books but Chyna was no longer the

20-year-old girl that wrote Me and My Boyfriend. She no longer was attracted to dope dealers or wished to be a trap queen. She was 33 years old now and trying to navigate her career out of the literary industry.

She desperately wanted to work in television and film. Chyna dreamed of being in front of the camera and behind it as well. She just hadn't figured out how to make her dreams come true. She'd gained a little recognition after meeting one of her favorite singers; Brandy. No one knew except her family and friends that she'd actually worked briefly with the singer's fiancé. She was flown out to L.A. to meet with a Hollywood agent and execs.

Chyna pitched several different show ideas and was in talks for several different television hosting jobs but nothing came of it. Disappointed, she started back at square one. But none of that mattered now. She had a book that needed to be written. Now that she was no longer signed to a major publication company, Chyna was her own boss. She had it scheduled for her next book to be released by August but here it was almost the end of May and she hadn't written a word.

Chyna hadn't expected it, but India's absence was affecting her tremendously. India had only been gone a week and Chyna felt like a piece of her had died. The silence of being alone in her three-story home was really beginning to bother her. She didn't know how she was going to survive being alone for three months.

If the last few days were any indication of how the next few months were gonna be, then Chyna's summer was going to be filled with drunken sex-filled nights. She wasn't ready to face the reality that India being gone for the summer was only foreshadowing that she'd be gone for good in the next three years. Chyna still hadn't come to terms that Tyreik was gone and never coming back. The spirit of him haunted her daily.

She couldn't escape him or that fatal day no matter how hard she tried. Tyreik was always there. He lived inside her. He was in her dreams, her thoughts. The smell of his cologne lingered in the clothes he left behind. A picture of them still sat on her vanity. Seeing his face everyday only reminded her of how much her life was in turmoil.

Every day she woke alone made her regret the way she reacted and carried on that day. The accident was all of her fault. Now she had to suffer through knowing he was gone because of her. She'd never be able to take her words back or redo the mistakes she'd made. Everything was set in stone. She was still alive yet alone.

It wasn't what she wanted but it was the hand she'd dealt herself. Realizing that smoking weed was only making her anxiety worse, Chyna placed the blunt into the ashtray. She needed to talk to someone. She needed company. Chyna grabbed her phone and called her ride or die, Brooklyn aka Brooke. Her and Brooke, along with her other best friend, Asia, had been friends since they were kids.

They had a lifelong friendship that spanned twenty-three years. Brooke and Asia were more than just her best friends. They were her sisters. They'd been through it all together. They'd survived beef, death, infidelity, motherhood and relationships. She needed them like she needed air to breathe. They were the only people on earth she trusted. Brooke and Asia hadn't failed her and never would. They kept her sane.

Brooke answered the phone on the fourth ring. She was in her car driving. She'd just gotten off work. Brooke was a human resource worker. During the day she was all business. She was prim and proper, but at night, she was the turn up queen. She loved a stiff drink and a good, hood, rap song. The business suits were put up and the low-cut shirts that showed off her exquisite tits came out. She was Chyna's party buddy. At that moment, Chyna needed her friend. She had to get out of the house before she lost her mind.

"What's up?" Brooke asked placing her on speakerphone.

"Shit. I'm trying to get out tonight. You down?"

"Chyna, it's Wednesday. You know I gotta go to work tomor. Besides, we just went out last night."

"And we kicked it too. C'mon, you know you wanna go."

"Go where?" Brooke sighed.

"Mandarin. They're having something tonight."

"I don't know, friend. I'm kind of tired."

"You tried and I'm pissed. You know that dude I left wit?"

"Yeah, he was cute. How was the dick?" Brooke yawned.

"Limp," Chyna chuckled. "And after slangin' that wack-ass dick, do you know that nigga left me wit' the hotel bill?"

"What?" Brooke shrieked, slamming on her brakes.

"Yasssssss! We were in the muthafuckin' presidential suite at the Four Seasons, my nigga. I ended up having to pay two g's."

"Hell naw." Brooke shook her head.

"Bruh, I'm sick after that shit. A bitch needs several drinks. Now you see why you gotta go wit' me."

"Heffa, please. You mean go wit' me. I'm the one that's gon' have to drive," Brooke teased.

"C'mon," Chyna whined. "I'll buy you your first two drinks."

"Huuuuuh… a'ight but I'm not gon' be out all night wit' yo' ass."

The rooftop lounge at Mandarin Lounge was poppin'. The midnight sky up above showcased a zillion twinkling stars. A warm, May breeze kissed Chyna's skin as she sipped on a glass of champagne and swayed to the beat of Demi Lovato's *Cool for the Summer*. She could tell by the energy surrounding her that the night would be memorable. All of her troubles seemed like a distant memory. She was feeling right and looked like a million bucks.

Chyna Danea Black was a stunner. Her smooth, caramel skin glistened under the moonlight. After years of having long, wild, curly hair, she decided to chop her shit off. Her super short, black, pixie cut was styled to perfection. Chyna's round, doe-shaped eyes were highlighted by black gel liner and demi, wispie lashes. Her chiseled cheekbones were contoured to the gawds. Every time she grinned, her deep dimples exposed the sweet innocence inside her that she tired so desperately to hide.

Chyna had a face you couldn't forget. People often found themselves mesmerized by her. She was one of those people you couldn't take your eyes off. She was breathtakingly, stunningly beautiful.

Chyna's style game was always on point. She turned heads whenever she entered into a room. Her sumptuous, full lips were painted a crimson red. She looked cool and dangerous in a pair of black, Quay sunglasses, and a strapless, black, quilted, leather dress that stopped right above her knee. The zipper on the left side of the dress was unzipped to expose her bronzed, toned thigh. A simple yet sleek and sexy pair of Louboutin, six inch, 'So Kate' heels completed her look.

Chyna was killing the game and she knew it. Brooke was just as equally hot. Her short, blonde, buzz cut framed her heart-shaped face perfectly. She rocked a blush-toned, metallic, long sleeve crop top, matching midi skirt and blush-colored, gladiator-style heels.

"Girl, ole boy in front of us is on you." Brooke said into Chyna's ear as she sipped her drink.

"Who?" Chyna quizzed, scanning the rooftop.

"The Puerto Rican dude right in front of us in the white V-neck."

Chyna eyed the guy. Sure enough, he was staring her way. The look he was giving her told her that he wanted her in the worst way. He was cute and Chyna was feeling herself. The hard-hitting music, bubbly and sexy energy surrounding her drowned out the demons in her head. Chyna didn't care about anything else except for making herself feel whole. She wanted to feel useful... special.

"I'll be right back." She stood up and smoothed down the front of her skirt. "Watch my purse for me." She requested as she and the guy linked eyes once more.

Subtly, Chyna gave him a head nod towards the fire escape. The guy placed down his drink and followed her. When he made his way outside, he found her leaning against the brick wall staring off into the distance.

"What you lookin' at?" He asked, looking in the same direction as she was.

"That's for me to know and you to find out."

"Damn, it's like that?" He grinned.

"Yep." Chyna glided her index finger down the side of his face.

"What you call me out here for then?" The guy placed one hand on the wall and leaned forward.

His lips almost touched hers.

"You know why." Chyna whispered feeling her temperature rise.

Without hesitation, the guy went in for a kiss but kissing wasn't something Chyna was interested in. She hadn't kissed a man since Tyreik and vowed that she never would. Kissing was way too sacred and personal. Kissing was a straight connection to the heart. No man would ever get that close to her heart again. Chyna turned her head and allowed his lips to meet with the side of her face.

The bass from the music inside the building thumped up against her back as she lifted her leg. The guy placed his strong hands on her thigh and raised her skirt. Chyna caressed his back and made her way around to unzip his pants. Boldly, she placed her hand inside his boxers. Chyna had to test out the merchandise before she purchased it.

Ole boy was working wit' a monster. Chyna eased down his jeans so he could gain access to her honeycomb hideout. The dude made love to her neck with his tongue and moved her panties to the side. To Chyna's surprise, he tried to slide his dick in her without a rubber.

"I might be easy but I ain't no dummy. You need to strap up, homie," she ordered.

The guy rolled his eyes and groaned before pulling out a magnum. Once he was strapped up, Chyna allowed him inside. The feel of his thick cock rocking in-and-out of her pussy filled every void in her life. Here she was, up against the wall with her skirt hiked up and pussy being rocked to sleep. Each thrust of his dick and scrape of brick on her back was the epitome of pleasure of pain.

Chyna was completely uninhibited. She wasn't the type of girl that needed a title of a relationship to sleep with a guy anymore. The old Chyna from when she was young and wildin' out was back and in full effect. Being faithful and dedicated to someone got you nowhere.

Giving someone your all only led to heartbreak. Fuck giving a fuck about someone else's feelings. The feelings that mattered were hers and her daughter's.

A man would never be the center of her world again. Chyna was happy that the loud music inside the lounge muffled her moans of ecstasy. Ten minutes later, it was over. The euphoric high instantly vanished and she quickly remembered she'd be going home alone and not to Tyreik or India.

"That was crazy. You a wild girl, mami." The dude grinned, zipping up his jeans. "What you on after the club let out? You wanna go have breakfast? Let me get to know you a li'l better?"

"I'm good." Chyna situated her skirt. "This was nice tho." She patted him on the chest.

"Hold up." He pulled her back by the arm.

Chyna shot him a look that could kill. She didn't like anyone grabbing on her.

"Excuse you." She snapped with an attitude.

"My bad, mami." He released her arm from his grasp. "I just wanna get to know you better. Can I please have your number?"

Chyna rolled her eyes and sighed. She hated when dudes begged. It was such a turnoff.

"Please, let me call you so we can go out to eat or something." The dude pleaded.

"Give me your phone." Chyna held out her hand.

She knew she wouldn't be able to get rid of him if she didn't give in and give him what he asked for. Annoyed, she placed her number in his phone. Back in the day she would've gotten away with giving him the wrong number but guys now-a-days dudes were slick. They'd call your phone right in front of your face to ensure you'd given the correct number. When he called, Chyna had every intention on not answering his call.

"You happy now?" She gave him back his phone.

"Yep, what's your name?"

"Chyna," she groaned, ready to go.

"Chyna what?" He asked so he could lock her number in his phone.

"Chyna Black." She turned to leave, done with the conversation.

"Bet, I'ma call you!" He yelled after her.

With a supermodel strut like she was on the catwalk, Chyna made her way back into the club. She didn't want hearts and flowers, promises of love and affection. Been there, done that. All of that was a lie. A dream being sold. She was a savage. She ate men up for breakfast. She wouldn't be tricked into believing that love was everlasting. Fuck a horse and a carriage. Chyna was her own savior. As she walked back over to Brooke; to her surprise, she spotted her jump-off from the night before.

"This muthafucka." Her nostrils flared.

Chyna stood frozen, shooting daggers at him with her eyes. He didn't even know she was watching him. He was too busy all up in some chick's face. Chyna felt bad for the girl. She had no idea that she was about to be his next victim. Fuming, she tried remembering his name but still couldn't. All she knew was that he looked like an ole light skin, R&B singing-ass nigga. There was no way she was going to be in the same spot as him and not give him a piece of her mind.

He had life fucked up if he thought he was going to get away with playing her. Ready for revenge, Chyna stomped towards him. On her way over she grabbed a random drink off a table. Her one-night stand didn't even see her coming. Chyna aggressively tapped him on his shoulder. Annoyed that someone was interrupting his conversation, he turned around aggravated.

"What?!"

Chyna reared her hand back and splashed the drink in his face.

"What the fuck?" The one-night stand yelled rubbing his eyes.

The alcohol was burning a hole in his eyes.

"Are you fuckin' crazy?" He rubbed his eyes with his shirt and tried to get a good look at the culprit.

"Than a muthafucka," Chyna spat.

"Umm, is this your girlfriend?" The girl he was rapping to asked, not wanting to be involved in a domestic dispute.

"No, boo-boo. I'm far from this lame-ass nigga girlfriend. I am however the chick he fucked last night then stiffed with a $2,000 hotel bill. This lousy muthafucka out here flossin' like he got big bank but ain't got shit. He's a bitch so don't waste your time trying to get the D, girl. It ain't worth it. Ain't that right, limp dick?" Chyna placed her hand on her hip and rolled her neck.

"Yo, this bitch is crazy! Don't believe shit she say!" The guy strained his eyes to see.

"Fuck you!" Chyna snatched the drink the girl was drinking and tossed it in his face too.

"Ahhhhhhhhhhh!" The dude screamed, blinded again. "Security! This bitch is trying to kill me!"

"You see. I told you. BITCHASSNESS!" Chyna mushed him in the forehead.

"Security! This crazy bitch is trying to blind me! I can't see!" The guy stumbled around unable to see.

A big, burly, white security guard came rushing over to see what the commotion was about.

"What's the problem?"

"She threw two drinks in my face! I barely even know this bitch! She's fuckin' insane! Get her away from me!" The Rotimi look-a-like continued to rub his eyes profusely.

"Ma'am, did you throw a drink in his face?" The guard asked.

"I sure did. And if I get my hands on another one, I'ma do it again." Chyna sucked her teeth.

"You're going to have to leave." The security guard grabbed her by the arm.

"Uh, excuse you. You better let me the fuck go!" She looked him up-and-down.

"Get yo' hands off of her!" Brooke rushed over.

"I don't know who you are but your girl gotta go." The security guard replied.

"This the muthafucka that ganked me last night!" Chyna pointed her finger at the guy like a gun. "Bitch-ass nigga!" She tried to kick him but missed.

"Oh word?" Brooke arched her brow. "This that nigga?"

Before anyone saw it coming, Brooke balled up her fist and punched him square in the nose. His nose instantly began to bleed.

"My nose!" Limp Dick cupped the blood that trickled like a stream from his nose.

"I need backup! I got two live wires on my hands!" The security guard said into a walkie talkie.

"You ain't gotta put us out. We out this bitch!" Chyna snatched her arm away. "Brooke, you got my purse?"

"Yeah, here." She handed it to her. "Let's get the fuck outta here."

Chyna gave Limp Dick one last look and stormed out of the building. Brooke was hot on her tail.

"Bitch, yo' ass is nuts! You just can't be poppin' off on a nigga without giving me a heads up first."

"My bad but I bet that muthafucka will think twice before he try to fuck over the next bitch."

"Now I'm even more lost and you're still so fine." – Beyoncé feat Drake, "Mine"

#3

Mariachi music played while Chyna sat outside alone at a table set for one. It was Memorial Day Weekend. All of her friends were out of town for the holiday. Once again, Chyna was left alone to face herself, which she found too difficult to do. She wasn't ready to admit that she was unhappy. For the last year and a half she'd been coasting along. She felt like her only purpose in life was to take care of India and write books so the bills could be paid.

Other than that, she felt like there was no need for her. Any happiness she had went out the door the day she lost Tyreik. Every time she opened her eyes, inhaled air to breathe, walked or talked, she regretted acting the way she did that fateful day. Each day she prayed to God to rewind time but time continued to march on.

There was no turning back. He was gone and she was left with wondering what they could've been. The only time Chyna felt fulfilled was when she was having sex. It was the only time she felt empowered and in control of herself. Sex made her feel alive and free. The only drawback was that after she came down from the orgasmic high, reality always set back in.

That Friday night she escaped the confines of her home to have dinner at one of her favorite Mexican restaurants: Rosalita's Cantina. The place was known for its margaritas and tableside guacamole. Soft, amber lights hung above creating a sensual glow among the patrons. The patio was filled with people eating, drinking and dancing. Some people sat at tables while others stood in groups and chatted.

Chyna sat in the center of the patio enjoying the scenery, her frozen strawberry margarita, and chips and salsa. The night air was thick and hot. Thankfully she'd dressed for the humid weather. Chyna wore her short, black, silky hair slicked to the back in a 1950's pompadour style. The diamond stud earrings Tyreik had bought her years before adorned her ears. She rocked a golden bronze beat with a super glossy lip. The red and black lumber jack button-up was unbuttoned all the way down to her navel exposing her ample, luscious breasts. A silver, tribal-inspired necklace decorated her décolletage.

The sleeves of the shirt were rolled up while the hem of the shirt was tucked inside a pair of super short, denim, booty shorts. Her lean, toned, caramel legs were on full display. Her signature, black, Louboutin 'So Kate' heels made her legs look longer than they actually were. Chyna was only 5'2. Silver bangle bracelets were stacked on each of her wrists. Her bag of choice that night was a black, Chanel, quilted, jumbo flap purse.

Chyna never stepped out of the house without looking like a million bucks. She'd lost twenty pounds over the last year and a half and felt damn good about herself. Looking good always brought out her inner vixen. Comfortably leaned back in her seat, she crossed her legs and surveyed the crowd. She was always searching for inspiration for her books. So far she hadn't found any but the night was still young.

The only thing interesting that had happened that night was somebody calling her phone private. Chyna didn't answer private calls so whoever it was would die before she picked up the phone. Chyna lifted her drink and placed it up to her lips. The cold chill from the glass sent a shiver up her spine. She thoroughly enjoyed the potent fruity flavor sensation of the slushy drink sliding down her throat. As she licked her upper lip, she couldn't help but notice a familiar face from across the way. Her heart instantly stopped beating. It was Carlos. Carlos Christianson was his name but everybody called him Los.

She hadn't seen or heard from him in a year and a half. When she decided to give her and Tyreik another chance, she stopped answering his calls. He'd run across her mind several times. She'd thought about him often as a matter-of-fact but figured he would never wanna hear from her again. Carlos was always the one that got away. He was the only guy besides Tyreik to have a hold on her. The chemistry they had was crazy.

He brought up emotions inside of her that she didn't even know existed. Chyna tried to steady her breathing as their eyes connected. He was still as fine as he was the last time she saw him. Hell, he looked even better. Carlos was one fine-ass white boy. He stood posted up wit' his mans with a cup of brown liquor in his hand. The Cuban cigar he puffed on gave him the appearance of being a Mexican drug lord.

Standing tall at 6'3, he had a muscular, athletic build. He wasn't too big or small. Carlos was just right. Like her, his hair was slicked back but his hair was shaved fairly low on the sides and tapered. His strong brows hovered over his hazel, diamond-shaped eyes. Carlos had a face that rivaled any male model on the runway. The five o'clock shadow he rocked highlighted his beautiful smile and pearly white teeth.

He donned three thin gold chains; one with a small cross pendant, one with an angel and the other with a Jesus piece. His outfit was simple yet swagged out. He wore a white, Yeezy V-neck tee, fitted, dirty wash jeans and Tims. His right arm was filled with a sleeve of tattoos and a Cartier watch. His left arm had a slew of tattoos as well. She could even see a glimmer of tattooed artwork peeking through the neck of his shirt. Carlos was tatted up. He even had tattoos on his hands.

There were no other words to describe him besides gorgeous. Since Tyreik, Chyna had encountered a lot of men. All good-looking but Carlos was of a different breed. She wanted him in the worst way. Seeing him again made her realize how much she missed his presence in her life.

During one of the toughest times in her life, he was a ray of sunshine. She never wanted to take her eyes off of him. Carlos' eyes bore into her skin. Her wish didn't come true. Some cornball rockin' a Gucci logo bucket hat, matching Gucci logo tracksuit and sneakers obstructed her view.

"Sweet lady, would you be mine? Sweet love for... a lifetime." He sang taking her perfectly manicured hand in his.

The dude had balls of steel. Before Chyna realized what was happening, he placed his dry-ass lips on the outside of her hand and kissed it. Chyna was appalled and disgusted. All she could concentrate on was the mouth full of gold teeth he had in his mouth. Homeboy's mouth was shining bright like a diamond. Chyna wanted to throw up.

"Ah uh, the devil is a liar." She quickly withdrew her hand.

"You mind if I have a seat?" He sat down before she could reply.

"I'm a lesbian." Chyna blurted out to get him to go away.

"That just means we can add another body to the bedroom." He ran his tongue across his upper teeth and grinned devilishly.

"Please don't make me cut you." Chyna closed her eyes and shook her head.

"You ain't gotta be so mean, baby girl. Your future husband is here." He raised his arms.

"I'm not mean, Satan. I'm saved. Jesus is my bae."

"I love the Lord too, girl. You know he say, he who finds a down-ass chick finds a good thing. Well, girl, after meeting you I think I done hit the lottery!" He slapped her on the thigh.

"I will shoot you," Chyna warned, ready to go off.

"Goddamn, girl, you look like dessert. I wanna sop you up with a biscuit!" The pest clapped his hands excitedly. "Girl, I would give you my whole paycheck! If I had job."

"Jesus, be a fence." Chyna looked up at the sky. "I'm about to go to jail."

"Tell me," The guy scooted his chair closer to hers and placed his hand on her knee. "Can I click yo' mouse? Can I refresh yo' page? Can I download yo' document?"

"If you don't get yo' ass away from me!" Chyna swatted him in the head with her clutch purse.

Bewildered, Gucci man blocked her hit with his arms. Chyna hit him so hard that her clutch flew open and all of her belongings dropped to the ground.

"I like that gangsta shit, girl." The guy growled turned on by her aggression.

Chyna was beyond pissed now.

"Oh my God! Where is the police when you need them?" She hissed, bending down to pick up her things that were sprawled all over the ground.

"I got it, baby girl." The dude tried to help her.

"Don't you touch none of my shit!" Chyna picked up her Anastasia Beverly Hills liquid lipstick, iPhone, cash and compact mirror.

She was so mad that she didn't even spot her house keys under the table.

"Babe." She heard a deep, raspy voice say just as she was about to get up and leave. "Is there a problem?"

Chyna looked up and found Carlos standing before her. All the air in her lungs escaped.

"You a'ight?" He asked wrapping his arm around her neck.

The scent of his sweet, hypnotic Tom Ford cologne almost made her cum on herself.

"No, but now that you're here I am." She intertwined her fingers with his and played along.

"This dude bothering you?"

"Yeah, I told him I had a man." Chyna shot the guy a evil stare.

"You said you was a lesbian!" The Gucci bandit shouted. "Over here turning me on for nothing!"

"Nah, this my girl, homie. You gon' have to fallback." Carlos turned Chyna's face towards his and kissed her on the lips passionately.

Chyna's entire body went limp. She hadn't kissed a man on the lips since Tyreik. She'd made it her business not to. She wanted to slap fire out of Carlos for being so forward but her mouth welcomed his warm, sweet tongue with ease. His cocky advances turned her on to the fullest. *Blue Ivy, help me,* she thought as he released his lips from hers.

"Y'all just nasty. You ain't have to do all that in my goddamn face. Shit, I mean she fine but she ain't all that." The dude stood up disgusted.

"Whateva, be gone." Chyna flicked her wrist, offended by his comment. "I ain't fine? Lies you tell!" She screwed up her face as he walked away.

"You done?" Carlos chuckled as he placed his drink on the table and sat opposite of her.

"Yeah." Chyna rolled her eyes and focused her attention on the gorgeous creature before her. "Hi." She smiled shyly.

"Hi." Carlos spoke back, captivated by her striking beauty.

Chyna inhaled deep. All of a sudden she felt super nervous. She didn't know if it was the slew of margaritas she'd already consumed or the pink part of her heart that had her acting girly but she needed to dead that shit immediately.

"How you been?" Carlos asked making himself comfortable in his seat.

"Good," she lied. "You?"

"I'm good." He lied too.

An awkward silence swept over them as they both tried to avoid eye contact. There was so much that needed to be said but neither of them was willing to bring up the past.

"Now say thank you." Carlos folded his right leg over his left.

"Say thank you for what?"

"For saving yo' pretty-ass." He smiled wide, revealing the two gold teeth on the side of his mouth.

"Who said I needed saving?" Chyna questioned, perplexed.

"I could tell by the look in your eye that you needed me." Carlos said with a hint of sarcasm.

Chyna wanted to deny that he wasn't telling the truth but she couldn't. For some odd reason, she felt like he was the missing piece of her fucked up puzzle.

"Did you know that guy?" He quizzed.

"Nah," Chyna screwed up her face. "Do I look like I would associate with someone that look like that," she scoffed.

"Actually, you do," Carlos teased.

"Shut up!" Chyna threw her napkin at him. "He was gettin' on my damn nerves. I'm like, dude, stop it. It ain't happening. Like, how dare he think that it's ok to try to talk to me? Like, do I honestly look like I would be the type of chick that would fuck wit' a dude like that? I mean, I was highly offended." She crossed her legs feeling her cunt.

"Be quiet. He's gone now." Carlos waved her off.

"What you mean be quiet?" Chyna asked unsure if he was being serious or playing.

"You sound kinda crazy right now. The Chyna I remember wasn't so stuck on herself. Where that girl at? 'Cause this new version of you is hella wack." He said turned off by her stuck-up behavior.

"Did he really just come for me?" Chyna looked around confused. "Umm, excuse you? Didn't nobody tell you to come over here and play Captain Save A Ho. I could've handled it myself," she spat.

"What was you handling, gettin' groped? From where I was standing, it didn't look like you were handling shit. So say thank you instead of poppin' off with a bunch nonsense." Carlos checked her.

"Whooooo are you talkin' to?" Chyna died to know.

Carlos had her so fucked up.

"You but I can go if you want me to. It's not a problem." He went to get up.

"Sit down." Chyna quickly pulled him back down.

For the life of her she didn't want him to leave. She wasn't expecting their conversation to go left so quick but she knew she was partly to blame. Putting her attitude on pause, Chyna examined him. There was an undeniable edge to Carlos that wasn't there before. She could tell by the dark look in his eyes that something traumatic had changed him. He seemed angry and withdrawn.

Whatever was troubling him, Chyna related to his pain. A part of her felt like she contributed to whatever plagued him. She hadn't treated Carlos right. She'd cut off all communication without any explanation. At the time she felt it was best but now that he was right there, live in the flesh, she realized she'd made a huge mistake.

"I don't say this very much but I'm sorry." She spoke barely above a whisper.

"Sorry for what?" Carlos asked perplexed.

"For ending things the way I did. You deserved better than that." Chyna looked down at her fingers instead of him.

Being vulnerable was not her forte.

"You good. Ain't nobody trippin' off that shit. That's old news." Carlos lied, unable to give her eye contact as well.

He'd dreamt of running into her over and over again. He had it all planned out. He wasn't going to give her the time of day. But as soon as he saw her face he was instantly drawn back into her web.

A small corner of his heart despised her for giving him hope back then and then ending things so abruptly. He truly believed at the time that Chyna was the one. Now he didn't know what to think of her. All he knew was that a year and a half later, his heart still beat erratically because of her. He hated the effect she had on him. Everything about her was imperfectly perfect. Her round, brown eyes captivated him. Despite all the time that passed, she was still his Achilles heel.

He could tell by the intense glare in her gaze that she'd changed for the worse. There was a lost look in her eyes. She looked like she was searching for something she'd never be able to find. Carlos knew he had no business even talking to her but he couldn't get up and walk away if he tried.

"Me and my pot'nahs about to head out. You wanna roll?" He asked eyeing her succulent thighs.

Chyna felt his eyes boring into her skin. She had no choice but to take a deep breath. She had to remain unbothered. She couldn't show that he made her nervous.

"Sure." She stood up and grabbed her clutch.

Chyna towered over Carlos as he sat sipping on his drink. The print of her pussy was right in front of his face. Carlos licked his bottom lip and cocked his head to the side. He was thoroughly enjoying the view in front of him. He wanted nothing more than to take off her shorts and wrap her legs around his neck. Chyna followed his gaze and realized he was staring at her box.

"You see something you like?" She popped her hip to the side.

"Yep." He leaned forward and kissed the face of her pussy through her shorts.

The heartbeat inside of Chyna's clit pounded like a bass drum. If Carlos kept this shit up, she was sure to fuck him right there in front of everyone. Carlos rose to his feet. He now towered over her. Chyna swallowed hard as she bit into her bottom lip. The look Carlos was giving her made her uncomfortable. She wasn't in her element. He had all of the control and she didn't like it one bit.

"You miss me?" He spoke softly as he caressed her cheek with his thumb.

Chyna swallowed the huge lump in her throat.

"Yes."

"Tight jeans on so she feel my shit." –
PartyNextDoor, "Break From Toronto"

#4

The next few hours of Chyna's life were like a whirlwind. She and Carlos sped around the streets of St. Louis drunk off Hennessy and high off weed. His friends were in their perspective cars right by their side. She stood with her arms wide-open inside of his black Jeep Wrangler. The roof and the doors had been taken off. Chyna welcomed the rapid wind as it blew against her face. Travis Scott's *Antidote* bumped loud as Carlos switched lanes. This was exactly what both of them needed - to be free and uninhibited.

Carlos watched with a smirk on his face as Chyna danced along to the beat. Chyna hadn't felt this alive in a minute. Her short hair blew in the wind as she twirled her ass in a circle. Carlos took another swig from the bottle. He didn't give a fuck that he was drinking and driving. Drinking numbed his pain.

Having Chyna there wasn't such a bad distraction either. Maybe she was the thing that he had been missing, maybe not. Either way, he was going to enjoy the time he had with her. As they whizzed down the deserted streets the street lights danced in the moonlight. Chyna reached down and grabbed her red cup. She was immediately pissed when she realized it was empty.

"We need some more liquor!" She yelled over the loud music.

Carlos nodded his head and pulled into the nearest liquor store parking lot. His boys pulled up beside him. Everyone got out of their cars. In a matter of minutes, it immediately became a party. The turn up in the liquor store parking lot was lit. Carlos' pot'nahs consisted of several black dudes and a couple of white. Some of the dudes had chicks with them as well.

Chyna eyed the fleet of cars in the parking lot. There was a Camaro, Mercedes Benz AMG, F-150 and an Audi Coupe. All of his boys stood posted up outside of their cars getting blazed and talking shit. They were all dressed from head to toe in designer gear and jewels. All of them were attractive. But Chyna wasn't checking for any of them. For the first time in a long while she had eyes for only one person.

"You having fun?" Carlos linked his index finger with hers.

"Yeah." Chyna smiled brightly as they swung their arms back-and-forth.

Chyna felt like she was in an early 2000's music video. Carlos was the rapper and she was his leading lady. She couldn't stop smiling and blushing. Every time they linked eyes she wanted him more and more. *Bitch, this is not an episode of Dawson's Creek. Stop it with this fairytale bullshit,* Chyna quickly reminded herself and drew her hand back.

Carlos noticed how the energy between them had quickly changed but didn't let it deter him. He knew that Chyna was fragile. He was willing to take his time with her. He needed her to know that neither of them had anything to lose.

"Yo Los, where we heading after this?" His homeboy, L.A., came over and gave him a pound.

Chyna checked him out on the low. L.A. was fine. He was tall, had honey-colored skin, a low-cut with waves and a neatly trimmed, black beard. L.A. looked like a guy that had played sports his entire life. He reminded her of the rapper Dave East. He had a New York swag about him that turned her on. Chyna wasn't really into light skin dudes but L.A. was most certainly fuckable.

"Ryan was talkin' about heading over to his crib and going on the rooftop," Carlos answered.

"You gon' introduce me to your friend?" L.A. eyed Chyna up-and-down.

Carlos peeped his lustful glare and draped his arm around Chyna's neck. He had to let him know that Chyna was his.

"Chyna, this is L.A. L.A., this is Chyna."

"Hi; nice to meet you." She extended her hand for a shake.

"Nah, we gon' bring this in for a hug." L.A. pulled her into him and made her give him a hug.

"Well aren't you friendly." Chyna joked as he rubbed her back.

Carlos clenched his jaw. L.A. was doing the most. He was always extra; and normally Carlos tolerated his bullshit, but when it came to Chyna, all bets were off.

"A'ight, that's enough." He pulled Chyna back towards him.

"How long have you two been friends?" Chyna asked, peeping the tension.

"We went to school together." Carlos placed her in front of him and wrapped his arms around her waist.

Are these niggas playing a game of whose dick is bigger, Chyna thought. By the feel of Carlos' dick in the crack of her ass, he was winning.

"Yeah, we played ball together." L.A. added.

"Here." Carlos reached into his pocket and peeled off two one hundred dollar bills. "Do me a favor. Go grab us a couple of bottles."

He was over L.A. and Chyna's introduction. She
didn't need to know anything else about him. Plus, he was
done with L.A. salivating over her. L.A. always wanted
what he couldn't have. He most definitely wasn't going to
have any parts of Chyna.

Chyna gladly took the money and switched inside
the store. She could tell that Carlos and L.A. had some kind
of rivalry going on but that was none of her business. She
was only concerned with keeping her buzz going. Slowly,
she sauntered down the aisle. Bending over, she searched
the shelf. Little did she know but Carlos was right behind
her. He was videotaping her every move with his GoPro.
Chyna's body was a masterpiece. Her body was built for
the beach. He loved everything about her frame. Her
caramel skin looked great next to his olive-colored skin.

"You need help?" He asked.

Startled by his deep voice, Chyna jumped.

"Nah, I'm good." She stood up with a bottle of
D'USSÉ in hand.

Chyna turned around and faced him. She
immediately spotted the camera.

"What's up wit' the camera?"

"I wanted to get tonight on film. Who knows when I'll get to see you again," Carlos said seriously.

"Whatever." Chyna playfully pushed him.

"Nah, for real. The camera likes you." He filmed her physique.

"I never met a camera that didn't." She hit a couple of sexy poses.

Carlos couldn't even front. The camera wasn't the only thing that liked her. He wanted every part of her she was willing to offer. Chyna was irresistible. She possessed an undeniable sex appeal that drew him in. He hated that every fiber of his being wanted her to stick around beyond that night. He wasn't going to press her about it. His pride was too big for that. Plus, he had his own inner demons that would keep them apart.

He was no good for Chyna. His own selfish needs would always get in the way. He would never be able to give her anything beyond the present. Chyna gazed into his eyes feeling the exact same way. Carlos brought an unexpected happiness into her life that made her uneasy. She'd become used to being alone. She never got attached. She was used to loving them and leaving them. No man on earth would ever be able to say he had her mind or heart ever again.

She was going to bask in the essence of the moment they were sharing and keep it moving like usual. The liquor and weed mixed with Carlos had her on a different type of high. She was determined to spend the night with him. She couldn't go home alone again. Being with him helped numb her pain. She would face her inner demons tomorrow, during the daylight. She was going to live for today. Taking her fate into her own hands, she grabbed Carlos by the back of his neck and pulled him into her embrace.

Chyna hungrily bit into his bottom lip. She wanted to ride the wave he had her surfboarding on. Right there in the middle of aisle #5, their tongues collided like wildfire. The visual of them tonguing each other down was like something out of a movie. Chyna wanted every part of him. She was so caught up in the moment that she dropped the bottle of D'USSÉ on the ground. Shards of glass ricocheted off the linoleum floor.

Neither Carlos nor Chyna cared. They were wrapped up in each other's hold. Carlos pushed her back into the shelf. Bottles of liquor crashed to the ground. The store owner went insane. Carlos could hear him going ballistic but he was blinded by the magnetic taste of Chyna's tongue. Now that he'd gotten a taste of her, he'd never be able to let her go again. With one kiss he was addicted.

Carlos held her face in the palm of his hands and kissed her lips feverishly. He no longer had to imagine her being in his arms. Here she was live and in the flesh. The threat of the cops being called loomed around them as their hands roamed each other's bodies. Carlos would gladly risk going to jail. Nothing but God could stop this union. Chyna had lit a fire that neither of them was able to control.

"Didn't they tell you that I was a savage?" – Rihanna, "Needed Me"

#5

The next morning Chyna lay on her back gazing up at the ceiling. She was on a path of self-destruction but she couldn't stop herself. She'd completely got caught up in the spontaneous events of the night and let her heart overcloud her better judgment. The weed and liquor mixed with Carlos had her on an unexpected high. She should've fucked him and kept it moving. Yet here she was trying to regain her composure.

Sex was the only weapon she had in her arsenal to erase the pain in her heart. She never caught feelings or went back for seconds but Carlos had touched a piece of her heart that hadn't been tampered with since Tyreik.

Chyna tried to fight against it but Carlos refused to give her the typical after-the-club-fuck she'd become accustomed to. He fucked her soul. Carlos attacked her body with vigor. His stroke game sent her to unknown galaxies. She wasn't expecting long dick strokes from a white boy. Carlos' cock reached all the way to her lungs.

Throughout the night she found herself bracing for the next ripple effect of his lovemaking.

Each lick of his tongue on her skin was like a wave from the ocean washing over her. Chyna drowned in his touch. Tears escaped her eyes when he flipped her over onto her stomach and took her from behind. Carlos' pipe game was so magical it put her ass to sleep.

She hated that he even had her contemplating staying longer than usual. It was daylight and she hadn't budged. She should've been gone but the sight of him sleeping peacefully next to her kept her glued to his side. Chyna was way too comfortable in his crib.

It shocked her that he lived only a few minutes from her in the Benton Park area of St. Louis. Carlos owned a newly renovated, brick, row home. Everything was immaculate. There wasn't a thing out of place. He was very anal with his things. His bedroom had an industrial, sleek, wide-open feel to it. A stone wall separated his bedroom from his bathroom space. There were no doors anywhere.

His color palette was all cool tones. His place consisted of cream, tan, nude and grey shades. His platform bed was made of the finest wood you could find. On each side of the bed were matching nightstands. A huge floor-to-ceiling window was on the right of her. She wondered if his neighbors were able to see their sexual tryst from the night before.

Carlos even had an open closet. It was filled with color coordinated clothes and shoes. Every item was folded and hung as if they were on display in a department store. Carlos' crib was the exact opposite of hers. Chyna's home was clean but her closets looked a mess. Her clothes and shoes were thrown all over the place. Carlos was far more structured than she would ever be.

Ok, get it together, bitch, she said underneath her breath, sitting up. *It's time for you to go,* she picked up her phone and ordered a cab. Chyna tried to be quiet as she slid out of bed but Carlos stirred in his sleep as soon as she moved. The first thing he saw when he opened his eyes was the sight of Chyna slipping out of his bed. Her curvaceous frame shimmered under the light of the morning sun. She was perfectly crafted by God. He wanted to trace every crease, crevice and fold of her body with his fingertips.

"Where you going?" He asked sitting up on his elbows.

Chyna looked over her shoulder at him. *My God he's beautiful,* she thought. *How in the hell is he this fine and he ain't brushed his teeth yet?* She wanted to sink her teeth in his lips and ride him until night fall. *Uh ah, bitch. There will be no more of that shit,* she told herself.

"Home." Chyna placed on her thong.

"Damn, you was just gon' dip without saying goodbye?"

"I mean, exactly what is it that you want me to say? Thanks for the dick but I'm about to jet?" She scoffed zipping up her denim booty shorts.

Carlos ignored her sarcasm and checked the time on his watch. It was a little after 8:00am.

"You wanna go grab breakfast?"

Chyna took a quick glance at him. His silky, black hair was all over his head. The huge eagle tattoo he had defined his muscular pecks. On his left arm was a pin-up girl playing cards. On his right was an Italian flag and the initials D.C. The inner part of her that still had a heart wanted to rush back over and jump into bed with him. But the cynical part of her knew better. Chyna was damaged goods. She was a bad girl that cared for no man.

"So what's up? You wanna go or what?" Carlos ran his hand through his disheveled hair.

"Nah, I'm good." She stopped putting on her clothes and looked him square in the eye. "Listen, last night was cute. I had fun but... last night is all I have to offer. I don't date. I'm not trying to be in a relationship. I'm not tryin' to be wife'd up." She made air quotes with her hands.

"I've changed. I'm not the same naïve, broken-hearted, dying to be loved girl you met a year and a half ago. Monogamy isn't my thing anymore. I like to fuck. That's it. So let's not make this into something more than what it is."

Carlos furrowed his brows and glared at her. He wasn't at all impressed by her speech. In fact, he was turned off by it.

"You done?"

"Yeah," she replied buttoning up her top.

"I was just tryin' to be nice and feed yo' ass. We ain't gotta go eat." Carlos pulled the sheets from off of him and stretched his arms in the air.

Carlos' fat dick slapped against his thigh. Chyna's eyes focused in on his thick, juicy, fully erect penis. Her right leg went limp as her mouth watered. *What I'm gon' do, Jesus?*

"And last I checked, I ain't say shit about a relationship." Carlos stopped stretching. "You really feeling yo'self, ma. Fallback. I don't know what type of guys you used to dealing wit' but I was just tryin' to make sure you got something to eat. You look hungry," he shot dismissively.

Chyna stood speechless. She wasn't expecting to be told off by him. For Carlos to be white, he had more heart than most dudes she knew.

"No disrespect. I'm just in a different space in my life right now. And I didn't want you to get the idea that this would go any further than today." She tried to explain.

Chyna knew that it was fucked up to re-enter his life only to leave him high and dry all over again but she had to do what was best for her. Protecting herself was far more important.

"It's all good, ma." Carlos placed a dismissive kiss on her forehead. "You ain't gotta explain shit to me. But umm, do me a favor. Lock the door on your way out." He slapped her hard on the ass then left her standing there.

He didn't have time for Chyna and her childish-ass games. He had his own shit to deal with. Girls like Chyna were a fuckin' headache. Stunned that he'd dismissed her, she picked her face up off the floor, grabbed the rest of her belongings and left.

The hot, early morning, May sun stung Chyna's eyes as she made her way down Carlos' steps. The cab she'd ordered was in front of his door awaiting her. Chyna felt like such a skank for doing the walk of shame. It was something about daylight that made you feel less inhibited. She wished she had something to cover herself up with. The cab driver couldn't take his eyes off her barely there outfit. She never felt so underdressed in her life. Thankfully, the sound of her phone ringing distracted her thoughts. A huge smile spread across her face. It was her daughter calling. She missed India terribly.

"Hello?" She sang with glee.

"Hi, Mom!" India shouted animatedly.

"Hi, my baby. How is the trip going so far?" Chyna relished the sound of her daughter's sweet voice.

"Good, we're in London right now. What are you doing up this early? It's like eight something in St. Louis," India questioned.

Her mother was known for sleeping till the afternoon.

"Umm, I couldn't sleep so I decided to go wash early so I could get it over with," Chyna fibbed.

She wasn't about to tell her daughter that she'd spent the entire night high off the finest weed and getting her back cracked by a fine-ass white boy. As far as India knew, her mother was a perfect angel.

"I can't wait for you to come home, India. Mama misses you so much."

"Mom, I've only been gone a week," India laughed, rolling her eyes.

"I know but I'm just so used to you being home with me. I don't know how I'm going to survive the whole summer without you. It's been so lonely being home without you. I'm gonna lose my mind when you go off to college."

"You'll be fine, Mom. You have Brooke and Asia. Who knows, maybe by the time I leave for school you'll be ready to date again," India said hopefully.

"Chile please, dating is the last thing on my mind," Chyna replied as thoughts of Carlos entered her brain.

"Well look, mom, I just called to say hi. I have to go but I'll call you later, ok?"

"Make sure you do so I can make sure you're ok," Chyna insisted. "And you be safe out there, ok?"

"Ok, Mom, I love you."

"I love you too, Indy." Chyna said reluctant to hang up.

She didn't want their conversation to end. On the bright side, she knew she'd be able to talk to her that afternoon. Before Chyna knew it, the cab driver rounded her corner and parked in front of her building. She threw him a $10 bill and got out. Chyna searched her clutch purse for her house keys as she neared her door. The more she dug inside her purse, the faster her heart started to beat. Her keys were nowhere to be found.

"What the fuck?" She stomped her foot and gazed around in disbelief.

This was the last thing she needed. She didn't have the time nor the patience to be locked out of the house. *When in the hell did I lose my keys,* she wondered. Visions of her hitting Gucci Man with her purse flashed before her eyes. Chyna quickly called the restaurant to see if anyone had turned in her keys but the hostess said no. Thoroughly pissed, she called her landlord. To her utter dismay, she was met with a voicemail recording stating that her landlord would be out-of-town for the holiday weekend. Chyna's apartment building was privately owned. There was no leasing office so she was officially fucked.

"This is some bullshit," she groaned on the brink of tears.

Her second thought was to call Brooke. Outside of India, she was the only other person to have a key to her house. Chyna remembered that Brooke was out-of-town too.

"What the hell am I going to do?" She closed her eyes and massaged her temples.

Chyna paced back-and-forth along the sidewalk. Several people walked by and eyed her as if she was a street walker. Chyna ignored their disapproving stares and continued to think but someone was calling her phone private again. Pissed beyond belief, she answered the call.

"What? Who the fuck is this?" She barked.

"Who is dis?" A woman asked with a Puerto Rican accent.

"Bitch, you called my phone. You've been blowing my shit up all night. You don't know who you callin'?" Chyna shot ready to implode.

"Is dis Chyna?"

"Yeah, who is this?"

"My name is Selena. Is my husband Waymon with ju?" She questioned in despair.

"Who? I don't know no nigga name Waymon! You got the wrong number!" Chyna ended the call.

The last thing she needed was a bitch calling her phone over a nigga she didn't even know. Chyna had to figure out where she was going to rest her head that night. She only had cash on her. The cash she had on her wasn't enough for a hotel room. Hell, she could only afford a cheap meal with the money she had on her. She was stumped. She had no place to go for the next few days. Then a thought popped in her head.

She could go back to Carlos' place. Sure, she'd been an obnoxious asshole to him but he was her only option. She prayed to God that he'd hear her out and let her stay. With her phone on 5%, she called another cab and headed back to his crib. By the time she arrived back at his crib, he was already gone. Completely broke and in desperate need of food, Chyna sat on his steps. *Damn, I should've went to breakfast with him.*

The warm, May sun baked into her golden skin giving her a headache. She prayed he wouldn't be gone long. Over an hour passed by before he pulled in front of his house bumping Future's *Dirty Sprite 2*. Carlos parked his car and got out. Chyna inhaled deeply and rose to her feet. Using her hand, she wiped off the back of her shorts in case there was any dirt on them.

Carlos walked around his car with his eyes locked on her. Chyna felt so small under his powerful gaze. She wanted to run and hide but she had nowhere to go. Plus, she was captivated by how handsome he looked. Seeing him in the light of day only magnified his sex appeal. Carlos was dressed in a Supreme baseball cap, blue t-shirt, blue sweat shorts and white, Classic Reeboks.

It was the first time she paid full attention to the tattoos on his legs. Normally leg tattoos on a man turned her off, but on Carlos, it was fly as hell. A spider web covered his left knee and a bevy of wilted roses cascaded all over his right leg. His cocky swag was a recipe for destruction. Chyna welcomed the challenge.

Carlos cupped his car keys in his hand and shot her a death glare. Chyna had balls of steel to show back up at his spot after the way she treated him. He ain't have shit for her ass but hard dick and bubble gum. He couldn't even front though, the way the hem of her shorts cupped her thighs softened his demeanor a little bit.

"What you doing here?" He asked with an attitude.

"I'm locked out of my apartment." Chyna said softly.

"Sucks for you." Carlos walked up his steps and right past her.

"Tyreik, wait! Don't be like that!" Chyna stopped him by grabbing his arm.

A flashback of her grabbing Tyreik's arm the same way the day of the accident flashed before her eyes. Chyna swiftly let Carlos go as a cold sweat washed over her.

"Tyreik? Who the fuck is Tyreik?" He screwed up his face.

Chyna wiped the invisible sweat from her forehead and tried to decipher what had just happened.

"Yo, you wild, man. You gon' call me another man name for real?" Carlos said shocked and hurt.

"My bad. I didn't mean that. I meant Carlos." She shook her head and gathered her thoughts.

Now was not the time for the ghost of Tyreik to be rearing it's ugly head. She had enough stress in her life at the present moment.

"Look, I need your help." Chyna shifted from one foot to the other. "Can I please stay here until Tuesday? My landlord and my friend are both out-of-town for the holiday. I have no way of getting into my apartment."

"You better call your boy Tyreik," Carlos scoffed. "Let him help you out."

Chyna gritted her teeth and willed herself not to tear up. She refused to cry in front of Carlos. No man would ever get to see her in such a vulnerable state.

"Trust me, if I could call Tyreik I would but I can't," she responded bitterly. "Seriously, Carlos, I wouldn't be here if I didn't need you. I apologize for this morning. I was being a bitch for no reason. That wasn't right."

Carlos saw the sincerity in her apology and softened a bit.

"I'ma chalk it up to lack of home training," he joked. "But look, if I let you stay here, what I get out the deal?"

"Some ass," Chyna giggled.

"I'm good." Carlos waved her off. "Think of something else. "

"You tried it." Chyna laughed playfully hitting him on the arm.

"For real; what else you got to offer?"

"I'll make you a home-cooked meal," she bargained. "Look, we both know that this thing between us isn't going to be a long-lasting thing. All I'm asking is that you let me stay until Tuesday morning. After that, you won't hear from me again."

Carlos eyed her suspiciously. Chyna didn't look like the type that could cook. He would be gambling big by agreeing to let her stay 'cause he really wanted a home-cooked meal. If she couldn't burn he would be highly upset.

"You promise?"

"Yeah, asshole," Chyna grinned.

"A'ight, you can stay." Carlos placed his hand out for a shake.

Chyna jumped up-and-down with glee and placed her tiny hand in his. They fit perfectly together.

"Oh and one last thing," she added.

"What now?" Carlos groaned.

"Since I'ma be here a few days, I'ma need you to cop me a few things to wear and some toiletries. A bitch is broke too. I spent the last of my cash on a cab getting back here."

"What was that you said earlier," Carlos recalled, placing his finger up to his temple. "You don't do relationships, right? Well, I don't do shopping sprees." He laughed unlocking the front door.

"Come on, Carlos, don't do me like that," Chyna whined. "I can't stay in these clothes until Tuesday. People been looking at me crazy all day!"

"Sound like a personal problem to me."

"Well, cutie, I like your bougie booty." – Kanye West feat. Kendrick Lamar, "No More Parties In L.A."

#6

"You better be glad I got some place to be tonight or else yo' ass would be shit outta luck." Carlos shot Chyna an evil glance while starting up the car.

"I ain't gotta go," she said smartly.

"Where you gon' be at then?" He looked at her quizzically.

"Your place." Chyna placed on her seat belt.

"Shiiiiiit, I don't know you like that. You ain't staying up in my spot by yourself. You must be crazy," he scoffed.

"Eww, don't nobody want yo' shit." Chyna reared her head back and furrowed her brows.

"Just making sure," he laughed, pulling off. "I should make yo' ass drive."

"Shit, I will. I'll even sit on yo' lap while I do it." She winked her eye.

"Yo' hot-ass," he chuckled.

"Where you gotta be tonight?" She asked.

"My business partner is throwing his girlfriend a book release party." Carlos replied, jumping onto the highway.

"That's cool." Chyna looked at herself in the visor mirror.

Home girl was in desperate need of a wash-towel and a toothbrush. After a brief pause, Carlos took his eyes off the road and looked at her.

"Who's your business partner's girlfriend?"

"Her name's Scotland."

"That's what's up. I read one of her books. She's good."

"You still write books?" Carlos questioned.

"Yeah, I'm supposed to be writing my new novel now but the words just aren't coming," Chyna confessed.

"It'll come to you."

"I hope so," she sighed, not quite so sure.

Chyna was secretly jealous that someone else was having success at writing. She'd completely lost her love for the art form. She sometimes wondered if she'd ever get the hunger back.

"So you not gon' ask me what I do for a living?"

"No." she giggled, shaking her head. "That would require me gettin' to know you better, which I have no intention on doing." She said matter-of-factly.

"Who hurt you?" Carlos screwed up his face. "Were you bullied as a child? Was your daddy not around, 'cause yo' ass need a hug. I ain't never met nobody that just don't give a fuck about nothing."

"I give a fuck about a lot of things, just not what you do for a living. I'm not trying to be mean or anything but I just don't care to do the whole '*what do you do, what's your favorite food, what's your favorite color, song and dance*'. It's just not me," Chyna shrugged.

"And FYI, I was bullied as a kid and my father is very much in my life."

"If your mouth was anything like it is now, I can see why people wanted to beat yo' ass in school," Carlos teased.

"Whatever, I'm sweet as pie." Chyna smiled and twirled her index fingers inside her dimples.

Carlos looked at her angelic face and reminded himself that the woman beside him had a heart made of black coal. He couldn't get trapped in her web.

"So who is Tyreik? Is that the dude you were wit' when I met you?"

"Yeah." Chyna spoke softly, placing her shoulders back.

"Why y'all breakup? You was in love with that dude?" Carlos looked back-and-forth between her and the road.

A huge lump formed in the center of Chyna's throat. She could barely breathe. At any moment her eyes were going to fill with tears. This wasn't how she pictured her day going. She was already locked out of her place for the next three days with no clothes or money. She didn't feel like rehashing old memories of her and Tyreik.

"Things just didn't work out." She placed her elbow on the armrest and stared absently out the window.

Visions of a bloody Tyreik flipped upside down trapped inside his truck paralyzed her. Carlos wanted to press the subject but the far away look in her eyes told him to leave well enough alone. Chyna was suffering in a way that not even she could comprehend. Although she'd become blunt, domineering, cutthroat and unapologetic, flashes of her old self peeked through the shitty surface.

Carlos was a good reader of people. He could tell that underneath all of the bullshit was a confused, scared woman. He hated that he was digging her. There was something about her that was begging to be loved. Too bad he wasn't the man to offer her the love she so desperately needed. Love wasn't an option for Carlos. For the past six months he'd done nothing but concentrate on his new business ventures and date one bad bitch after another.

Like Chyna, he wasn't in the business of giving his heart to the opposite sex. He had a few women that he rotated when he wanted company. His main focus was getting bread. After what he'd gone through, nothing else mattered. He valued nothing. Some days Carlos felt like he was just coasting along.

He was existing in a world he didn't want to be in. He hadn't felt alive in months. Nothing or no one would cure the anguish he had in his heart. He was mad at himself, the world and most of all, God. But in the last 24 hours he felt like a brand new person. Chyna's sassiness intrigued him and made him smile.

A short car ride later, they pulled into a shopping plaza. The plaza was located in one of the worst areas on the South Side. Chyna looked around and saw a Shop 'n Save, Citi Trends, Dots, Rainbow and a Shoe Carnival. *No he ain't taking me here to buy no clothes,* she thought.

"Come on." Carlos placed the car in park.

"Excuse you? I'm not gettin' out of this car. I'm trying to live. My plans were not to get shot today."

"You must wanna stay in that outfit until Tuesday then," he shot.

"This is some bullshit." Chyna fumed getting out of the car.

She hated coming on that side of town. She didn't have anything of value in her purse but she still held it close to her chest. A lot of gang members and corner boys lived in that area and trolled the plaza. Chyna was not about that thug life anymore. She was a reformed hood chick. She would fuck a bitch up if need be but she tried to keep that part of herself on lock.

"Where we going?" She secured her arm with his for protection.

"Will you back up off me?" Carlos playfully yanked his arm away.

"No, 'cause if somebody try to step up, they gon' get to you first." Chyna looked around frantically.

"You sure you ain't white 'cause you actin' mad scary," he laughed.

"Shit, yo' people ain't scary no more. They will fight and kill a bitch with the quickness. Yo' people give zero fucks."

"I wish I could argue wit' that but I can't," Carlos responded sadly.

All of the senseless killings of black folks from the hands of white cops was infuriating.

"Which store we going in tho?"

"Dots." He pointed at the sign.

"You playin', right?" Chyna stopped dead in her tracks.

"No. You need some clothes, don't you?" Carlos looked at her like she was crazy.

"Do I look like a Dots kind of girl to you?" She eyed him up-and-down with disdain. "Look at my purse." She held it up so he could get a good view. "This is Chanel... not Chantell."

"Man, if you don't bring yo' bougie-ass on in here." He tried pulling her by the arm. "You ain't too good for a five dollar top. As a matter-of-fact, it look like you got on a five dollar top right now."

Chyna gasped, clutching her chest.

"How dare you? This shirt cost me a hundred dollars."

"Ninety-five dollars too much if you ask me. Now bring yo' pretty-ass on so we can get back to the crib."

Chyna flared her nostrils. When she suggested they go shopping, she didn't mean hitting up Ghetto-R-Us.

"You are tryin' my life right now." She popped her lips and stomped towards the store.

Carlos opened the door for her and held it open.

"See, you tryin' to be funny but I'ma make it do what it do, baby." Chyna switched past him.

Carlos couldn't help but check out her ass as she sauntered by. Chyna had a handful of ass that he couldn't wait to dive into again. She could feel his eyes on her ass so she switched harder. She had something to prove to Mr. Carlos Christianson. Dots wasn't her speed but she would make it work and rock the hell out of whatever he bought her.

"Hold this please." She handed him her clutch. "I got work to do."

Chyna attacked the racks of clothes with a vengeance. In a matter of minutes she was in the dressing room trying on items she picked out. Carlos sat idly by on a bench checking out pictures on Instagram. Dressed in her first outfit, Chyna opened the curtain and cleared her throat to get his attention.

Carlos took his eyes off his phone and gazed up at her. He'd never seen anyone make a cotton/spandex blend look so good. Chyna came out the dressing room in a white bandeau top and a camel-colored midi skirt. The skirt highlighted her round hips and plump ass. Carlos wanted nothing more than to peel the two items of clothing off her body.

"You like?" She stood on her tippy toes and spun around in a circle.

"You look a'íght." He tried to play it off like his dick wasn't brick hard.

"Let me find out you a hater." Chyna smiled before closing the curtain.

She noticed the flicker of lust in Carlos' eyes as he admired her frame. She thoroughly enjoyed every second of it. None of that mattered though because after the holiday, she would never see him again.

"Drink on the way so I can cope."

–Tank, "So Cold"

#7

Although her outfit cost a total of fifteen bucks, Chyna somehow looked like a million bucks. She rocked the hell out of her Dots outfit. She even got several compliments on it as Carlos introduced her to several of his friends. The book release party was in full swing. Knight was a gracious host and Scotland looked nothing short of stunning. Everyone was dressed in their best after-five attire.

To Chyna's surprise, the celebration was held at Knight and Carlos' restaurant called Fusion. Fusion was located in the heart of downtown St. Louis. The dishes were inspired by tastes from around the globe, including: French, Moroccan, Italian, Mexican and Asian. The restaurant held a massive bar, lounge, dining area and a patio. Colorful lights of all different hues hung from the ceiling. In the center of the bar was a huge, crystal chandelier that Chyna adored.

She was thoroughly impressed by the décor and the food. Everything she ate was immaculate. Carlos and Knight had outdone themselves. Never in a million years would she have expected Carlos to be a restauranteur. As Chyna mingled and chit-chatted with Carlos and his friends, she learned that Fusion was his third business venture. Carlos also owned two tattoo shops.

Chyna couldn't help but admire his hustle. It was one of the things she admired most in a man. Carlos was a cool guy. He was confident and cocky as hell, which she secretly loved. There weren't many men that could match her slick mouth but he stepped up to the plate each time. Plus, the man was drop-dead gorgeous.

The man knew how to clean up well. The black, Dolce & Gabbana, 3-Piece, shawl collar suit made of wool and silk was tailor-made to his body. The black, skinny tie he donned gave the look a mod 60's effect. Carlos was the epitome of sex appeal. Chyna caught herself on several occasions having to fan herself when she came in contact with him. She detested that he had that kind of affect on her. She never wanted a man past one night but there was something about Carlos that had her wanting more.

She watched closely as he maneuvered around the room shaking hands and making small talk. She hadn't seen a man command a room like that since Tyreik. Everyone was captivated by him. Every chick in the room was dying to get in his pants. Chyna felt good knowing she was the one going home with him that night.

"You having fun?" He asked handing her a glass of champagne.

"Yeah, your people are cool."

"I told you, I don't fuck wit' no lames." He shot her a sexy grin.

"How did yo' white ass get so hip?" Chyna eyed him genuinely perplexed.

"Oh, you asking me a personal question?" Carlos stood back shocked. "This what we do now? 'Cause I thought you ain't wanna know nothin' about me."

"I'm just curious, that's all." Chyna grinned, knowing she was contradicting herself.

"If you must know, I'm a first generation Italian American. I was born in St. Louis. I grew up in the Peabody

Projects. My parents ain't have shit when they moved here. I was raised with the work ethic of an immigrant but the hustle of a city kid."

"That's crazy." Chyna said stunned.

"It's so much more that I could tell you but gettin' to know each other ain't your thing, remember?" He shot sarcastically.

"Whatever." Chyna gave him a quick peck on his cheek.

Astounded that she'd shown an ounce of affection, Carlos took a sip of his drink then gently slipped his fingers between hers. Chyna looked down at their fingers intertwined. Her heart filled with emotions she hadn't felt in over a year. All signs were pointing to this is where she belonged. Looking up, she locked eyes with his.

A smile graced the corners of her pink-painted lips. Like any other time they were together, it was as if she and Carlos were the only ones in the room. He held all of her attention and vice versa. Carlos hadn't been able to take his eyes off her all night. Her supple, soft skin shined in her barely there outfit. The white bandeau top showcased her full, luscious breasts and toned stomach. The camel midi skirt hugged her curves effortlessly. The nude, strappy, open-toed heels he copped her accentuated her white, manicured toes.

Carlos could look at her heart-shaped face for the rest of eternity and never get bored. Her pixie cut framed her face flawlessly. He tried not to feel anything when they interacted but something about Chyna continued to draw him in. Carlos relished in the touch of her hand until he spotted his past walking in his direction.

He'd been told by Knight that his ex, Bellamy, wasn't going to be able to make the festivities. Yet here she was looking like hurt, lust and anguish wrapped up in a red bandage dress. Bellamy was dressed to kill and succeeding. Her long black hair was parted in the middle and hung straight to the back. Dramatic, winged liner accentuated her almond-shaped eyes.

Bellamy's Kylie Jenner injected lips were on full pout mode. Her 32 D's bounced as she strutted across the room. Carlos zeroed in on her round, Armenian hips as they swayed from side-to-side. He was so entranced by her presence that he didn't even realize he'd let go of Chyna's hand. Chyna noticed though. She never missed a beat.

She'd spotted Bellamy before he did. Bad bitches always peeped other bad bitches. Bellamy was beautiful. She reminded Chyna of the Instagram model Amrezy. She just wanted to know who she was and why she had the same effect on Carlos she did. With a glass of champagne in hand, Bellamy approached Carlos. Without a word, she wrapped her arms around his neck and gave him a warm hug.

Chyna stood back speechless. She didn't want to feel some type of way but she did. There was an undeniable connection between the girl and Carlos. Chyna didn't like the shit at all. *This bitch gotta go,* she thought folding her arms across her chest.

"Hi, baby." Bellamy closed her eyes and held Carlos in her arms.

"What's up wit' you?" He replied, unsure of how to feel.

He hadn't seen Bellamy in six months. The last time they'd seen each other was nothing short of unpleasant. They'd both said things that could never be taken back.

"Long time no see." Bellamy finally let him go and side-eyed Chyna.

"Yeah, I didn't think you were coming." Carlos cleared his throat.

"I wasn't but my schedule ended up clearing up, so here I am. And here you are…" she looked Chyna up-and-down.

The evil glare Bellamy was giving Chyna prompted Carlos to introduce the two women to each other. For a second he'd forgotten that Chyna was there.

"Bellamy, this is my friend Chyna. Chyna, this is my ex Bellamy."

Friend, Chyna thought insulted. Yeah, technically they were just friends. She'd made it perfectly clear that she wanted nothing more than that. Secretly she hoped that he looked at her as more than a friend; she did.

"Hello." She extended her hand to Bellamy for a shake.

"We dating chicks that wear cheap outfits now?" Bellamy asked Carlos instead of shaking Chyna's hand.

In Bellamy's eyes, Chyna was the enemy. There would be no pleasantries. She was with her man and Bellamy didn't do too well with competition. Despite the fact that she and Carlos were no longer together, they had a long history. He would always be hers. No other woman would ever take her place in his heart.

"Oh, ok." Chyna chuckled drawing her hand back.

She'd totally forgotten that she was in an inexpensive frock. Bellamy's diss didn't shake her one bit. She'd met chicks like Bellamy before. Bellamy thought 'cause she and Carlos shared a past that she was entitled to him forever. Chyna got it. She understood why Bellamy was mad. She'd be mad too if she allowed a man like Carlos to slip through her fingers. But Bellamy's leftovers were Chyna's entrée. She was going to get so full off him that there wouldn't be anything left of him for anyone.

Bellamy had fucked up and let Carlos fall into the right bitch's hands.

"I texted you a few weeks ago. You didn't respond back. Did you get my message?" Bellamy quizzed, pissed.

"Yeah, I did." Carlos responded with an even tone.

"So you just didn't respond?" Bellamy said visibly hurt.

"Nope." Carlos said coldly.

"Ok." Bellamy inhaled deeply. "Well, I just came over to say hi. Enjoy your night, Los." She leaned forward and placed a sensual kiss on his cheek.

"Nice meeting you, Shrimp Lo Mein." Bellamy shot Chyna an unconcerned glance before walking away.

"Giiiiiiiiirl, don't make me beat yo' ass," Chyna laughed ready to turn up.

Bellamy tossed her hair over her shoulder and kept walking.

"Well that was awkward." Chyna gushed, finishing off the last of her drink.

"Tell me about it." Carlos signaled for the waiter.

He needed a quick pick-me-up after that unexpected encounter with Bellamy.

"She's pretty. Bitchy but pretty," Chyna stated as the waiter came over.

"Bellamy's a lot of things." Carlos handed her another glass of champagne.

"How long were y'all together?"

"Fifteen years." Carlos downed his entire glass.

"Damn, that's a long time." Chyna gulped realizing she had stiff competition. "Is it over or is there still a chance y'all might get back together?"

"Nah, it's a wrap on us." Carlos shook his head. "We just friends."

Chyna let out of sigh of relief. She didn't even know she'd been holding her breath the whole time she was waiting for his reply.

"Excuse me. Can I get everyone's attention," Knight yelled clicking a butter knife against his champagne glass.

All of the partygoers gathered around. Knight stood in front of the room. He was a tall drink of chocolate milk. All of the women in the room swooned over him but he only had eyes for Scotland.

"Come here, baby." He held out his hand for her.

Scotland nervously tucked her hair behind her ear and stood by her man's side. She and Knight were the picture-perfect couple. They complimented each other well. Chyna could tell by the way they gazed lovingly into each other's eyes that they were madly in love.

"First off, on behalf of Scotland and I, I want to thank you all for coming tonight. It means a lot to us that you were able to be here to celebrate with us. Y'all know me and Scotland have been through it—"

"Yes, we have." Scotland shook her head.

"But me and my baby made it through," Knight continued.

"Look at God. Won't he do it?" Scotland faked having the Holy Ghost.

Everyone cracked up laughing.

"You stupid, man." Knight couldn't help but laugh too. "Anybody that knows me knows that I'm not one to get off into my feelings. But I must say that when you find something good, don't let'em go. Scotland is my something good. She's my heart. I knew she was going to be my wife the first moment I laid eyes on her. I couldn't imagine my life without her. So, I say all that to say." Knight bent down on one knee.

"Will you marry me?" He asked opening a Neil Lane box with an emerald-cut diamond and platinum ring inside.

Tears of joy rushed down Scotland's cheeks. She was truly shocked. She had no idea that Knight was going to propose to her.

"Hell yeah!" She jumped up-and-down with glee.

"I can't wait to spend the rest of my life wit' you, babe." Knight placed the ring on her finger and gave her a loving kiss on the lips.

Carlos glanced over at Bellamy. She sipped on a glass of champagne and looked back at him. Feelings of loss echoed in each of their eyes. There were so many things that were still left unsaid between them. Carlos exhaled heavily and turned his attention back to Chyna. He hoped that she hadn't caught him making eye contact with Bellamy. She hadn't. He quickly noticed that she wasn't even clapping. The change in her demeanor was evident. Sorrow radiated off of her.

Chyna choked back the tears that were rising in her throat. Seeing the love Knight had for Scotland melted her heart. As he spoke, she wished nothing more than that it was her in the front of the room. If things were different, it would've been her being proposed to. The whole time she and Tyreik were together she wanted nothing more than for him to propose to her. They'd talked about marriage often but he always had an excuse as to why the time wasn't right. Now that day would never come.

"You a'ight?" Carlos asked, wondering what the problem was.

"Yeah, I'm good," Chyna sniffed, pulling herself together.

"You sure?"

"Yeah," Chyna lied.

There was no way in hell she was going to tell him what was going on with her. On the real, she'd had enough excitement for one day. Between losing her keys, his sour-puss face ex and the proposal, she was emotionally exhausted. For the rest of the night, Chyna was super quiet. Carlos tried to get her back in a good mood but Chyna wasn't having it. The only thing she wanted to do was go back to his crib and go to sleep.

"'Cause the scars on your heart are still mine." – Rihanna, "Woo"

#8

After another hour at the party, Chyna got her wish and they went home. The entire car ride back to Carlos' crib was filled with silence. So many *what-ifs* and *whys* flooded her mind. She never envisioned that at the age of 33 she'd be single and depressed. She thought by now she'd be married and on her second child. But God had other plans. Just as she'd feared, Chyna was alone - just like her mother.

Her mother, Diane, had driven everyone that mattered in her life away with her entitled, know-it-all, hard-headed ways. Here Chyna was doing the exact same thing. She never wanted to end up like her mom but with each day that passed, she was becoming her exact replica. Chyna didn't want to pass the negative trait onto her daughter. She wanted India to be loving, caring and giving but not naive. She didn't want her to become bitter, cynical and cold like Chyna and Diane.

Back at Carlos' place, she walked silently to his bedroom. The first thing she did was take off her heels. Her feet were killing her. Four and a half inch, cheap heels weren't the best thing to be standing in for hours at a time. Carlos loosened his tie and entered the bedroom space. He found Chyna sitting on the side of his bed with her hands cupped under her chin. She was so deep in thought that she didn't even notice him standing there.

"Ay yo, you good?" He slid his tie from around his neck.

He was honestly concerned for her well-being. Chyna blinked her eyes and came back to reality.

"Yeah." She finally answered. "Umm." She stood up. "I'm about to take a bath. Do you have a t-shirt or something I can put on?"

"Yeah," Carlos opened his dresser and handed her a white, V-neck tee. "You need anything else?" He was willing to do anything to make her feel better.

"Nah, I'm okay. Thank you though." Chyna slipped around the corner to the bathroom and stripped naked.

In the past, she would've been highly nervous to bathe in an open space but after everything she'd been through, shit like that didn't rock her. Chyna slowly dipped her body into the tub. The steaming hot water soothed her bones. Carlos took off his suit jacket and laid it on the back of the couch. He needed an alcoholic pick-me-up. A cold beer would hit the spot.

He'd never seen Chyna so quiet and forlorn. Something about seeing Knight propose to Scotland really rattled her. If he'd known she would react that way, he would've left her at home. It was obvious that old love demons still haunted her core. Hell, they haunted him too. He thought he was done with his past.

After seeing Bellamy it was clear that they still had unfinished business. Carlos didn't want to tread those unsteady waters again. They'd done their best to make it work despite the circumstances. What they had was over. There was no going back but seeing her face brought back old feelings he thought he'd buried along with their son.

"Los!" Chyna called out his name.

Carlos looked over his shoulder at her with a sour expression on his face. She never called him Los. He didn't want her to start now.

"Yeah."

"I'm about to go to bed, if that's okay?"

"Yeah, sure," he nodded.

"Goodnight." She gave him a quick wave.

"Night." Carlos licked his bottom lip as she turned to leave.

His t-shirt barely covered her ass. Her plump cheeks bounced up-and-down as she tiptoed over to his bed. Carlos prayed to God he'd be able to touch her again before she left. He had to have her beneath him. He needed to hear her scream out his name as he took her to new heights of ecstasy. With the way she was acting, Carlos didn't know if that would even be an option or if he wanted it to be. Chyna had way too much baggage. He had a full bag too. Carlos hadn't dealt with his own shit. He didn't know if he had the energy to help her unload hers too.

"No-no!" Chyna tossed and turned. "No, Tyreik! Don't leave! Don't get in the car!" She screamed in her sleep.

Carlos lay beside her watching television, startled by her outburst.

"Chyna!" He tried to wake her.

"Tyreik! Tyreik!" She wailed so loud she woke herself up.

Tears streamed down her face as she sat up bewildered. Sweat dripped from every crevice of her body. She was a mess.

"Tyreik, come back!" She wept into the palm of her hands. "I'm so sorry."

"Chyna, stop crying." Carlos pulled her hands away from her face.

His heart was beating a mile a minute. He didn't know what to make of her erratic behavior.

"It was just a bad dream." He made her look at him.

Chyna gazed at his worried face then around the dark room. The television was the only thing that gave the room light.

"What is going on with you? What the hell happened between you and this Tyreik dude?" Carlos held her hands in his.

Chyna looked into his eyes. Her chest heaved up-and-down as she cried. She wanted to tell him everything but couldn't. It was too hard to relive the pain of that horrific day. How could she reveal that she'd ruined someone's life? She couldn't and wouldn't. She was already ashamed enough. She couldn't handle the disapproving look Carlos was sure to give her once he found out what she'd done. It was unforgivable.

"Chyna, answer me. What the hell happened?"

"I can't." She sobbed breaking her hands away from his grasp.

Chyna couldn't control her breathing. She felt trapped in her own skin. Her body was on fire.

"Yes you can," Carlos pleaded angrily.

"No, I can't." Chyna frantically rose to her knees and wrapped her arms around his neck.

All of the pent up anxiety, frustration and sadness inside her needed to be released. Sex with Carlos would cure the pang in her heart. Carlos wanted to protest. He knew sex wouldn't solve what plagued her but Chyna's lips met with his and everything faded to black.

Her sweet tongue glided against his with velvet ease. Carlos ran his hands up her spine and cupped the back of her neck. He had every intention on making Chyna forget the nightmare and Tyreik. Chyna straddled his lap and pulled his t-shirt up over her head. In a matter of seconds, their clothes were on the floor.

Her caramel breasts danced before his eyes. Carlos hungrily licked her nipples until they sprouted like rosebuds. Chyna arched her back. His tongue was torturing her nipples. She didn't know how much more she'd be able to take. She needed the D bad. The lips of her pussy ached for it.

"Fuck me," she panted heavily.

"Is that what you want?" Carlos palmed her ass cheeks and lifted her up.

"Yes." Chyna snapped her eyes shut as he entered her soaking wet slit.

There would be no condom that night. They both needed each other in a way a condom couldn't fulfill. Carlos needed to feel every inch of her. Chyna's wetness sucked him in as she glided up-and-down his pole. Nothing but the sounds of her moans and her ass slapping against his thighs could be heard.

"Oh my God! This shit feel so good!" Chyna screamed in sheer delight.

Carlos lay on his back griping her ass while flicking his tongue across her berry-colored nipples. He couldn't get enough of her. His dick grew harder with each stroke. Chyna's moans ignited a firestorm within him. He wanted to be inside her forever. Her ass bounced up-and-down on his shaft at an intense speed. Chyna was like a wild animal that couldn't be tamed. He was magnetized by it.

"Mmmmmm, Carlos! This dick feel so good! Fuck, I'ma cum!" She wailed on the brink of climaxing.

"You gon' take this dick! I'm not done fuckin' you!" He pumped in-and-out while holding her in place.

"Fuck!" Chyna moaned as he flipped her over onto all fours.

The side of her face was flat down on the mattress while her ass was pointed up in the air. Carlos was determined to fuck her so good she'd forget Tyreik ever existed.

"Oooooooh, baby," Chyna trembled trying to lie down on her stomach.

"Uh ah," Carlos slapped her ass cheeks. "Stick that ass up in the air!" He fucked her long and hard.

"Ahhhhhh... it's so big!" Chyna moaned.

With each stroke of his cock her titties slapped against her. Carlos could feel her about to cum. Gripping her right shoulder, he slammed his dick into her.

"You love this dick, don't you?" He groaned, rotating his hips in a circular motion.

"Yes." Chyna panted, orgasming. "Oh my God, yes!"

Cumming too, Carlos pulled his dick out and came on her butt cheeks.

"She brace herself and hold my stomach. Good dick'll do that." – Kanye West feat. Kendrick Lamar, "No More Parties in L.A."

#9

This... this is what I live for. Your... kiss... this is what I love for. Oh I...I could dream all night. No one. Why you so good to me? Chyna sang lost in the lyrics. Alex Isley's *Dreams in Analog* played throughout the entire house. Chyna could listen to Alex Isley's angelic, soulful, jazzy voice all day long and never get tired. Carlos had never heard of her but as soon as he heard her voice, he fell madly in love with her too. Her song *Don't Do* serenaded their souls as Chyna danced a slow groove while cooking.

It had been ages since she had a lazy Sunday where she did nothing but drink wine, have sex, laugh and play around. She and Carlos couldn't get enough of each other. Neither of them could keep their hands to themselves. After the nightmare debacle, Chyna was in dire need of some fun. So far it had been nothing but good vibes coming her way. She'd spoken to India which always brightened her day.

Her baby girl was having a ball. Chyna couldn't have been happier for her. India was experiencing things that Chyna had only dreamt of as a child. She felt good knowing that she was raising a daughter that would be will versed in so many things. Chyna knew she had many flaws. She could be abrasive, pigheaded and hard to get close to but a bad mother she was not. She gave India the world and was a better person for it.

As promised, she was preparing Carlos a home-cooked meal. For dinner they would be having Mexican corn on the cob with paprika and Feta cheese, grilled asparagus, bacon-Dijon mustard chicken breasts served over a bed of white rice. The aroma coming out of the kitchen was mouth-watering. Outside of his mother, no other woman had ever cooked for him.

Cooking was never Bellamy's forte. She found it way too difficult to do. It was effortless for Chyna. She fluttered around his chef-style kitchen without a worry. She was in heaven. Carlos had a kitchen that was made to be cooked in. He had stainless steel appliances. His kitchen island was made out of Calcutta stone imported from Jerusalem. Everything about it was striking.

Over the years, Chyna began a love affair with cooking. She loved to see the look on people's faces as they ate her food. Cooking was another creative outlet for her just as makeup and home decorating was. Through her YouTube channel she was able to express herself outside of writing. Chyna had to figure out what she was going to do with her writing career. It had become a job to her, a way to pay the bills.

Sometimes she felt guilty for not loving writing anymore. With no high school diploma she'd made a life for herself and her daughter. Through writing she'd experienced things most people would never be able to achieve. Chyna never wanted to spit in God's face. He'd been so generous with his love and mercy when it came to her.

She just wanted more. She wanted to spread her wings and show the world the other gifts she'd been blessed with. She was tired of being ganked by shady black publishers. Chyna had written books for Triple Crown Publications and Urban Books. It was a damn shame that she hadn't received a royalty check from TCP in over six years. The royalties she received from Urban was enough for dinner and a movie. It saddened her how black people could be so evil, greedy, and conniving.

Chyna often wondered what was all of her hard work for. She seemed to always end up on the losing end of the stick. She wanted so desperately to win and defy the odds. She wanted to see the fruit of her labor. There was no way that God had brought her all this way only for her to lose in the end. There had to be more in store for her. There just had to be.

Dressed in one of Carlos' wife-beaters, no bra and booty shorts, she took a sip of wine. The food was only minutes away from being done. After the all-night-fuck-session she and Carlos had, she was famished. Carlos watched her from the living area. He was in awe of her resilience. There weren't many people that could carry the burdens Chyna carried. She acted as if the night before had never happened. She'd grown good at pretending as if everything was alright. He recognized her act because he was camouflaging pain too.

"Time to eat." She beamed with pride.

Excited for him to taste her food, she placed his plate on the table next to hers. Chyna loved Carlos' dining room table. It was a Yaya & Wenge table made from African Yaya Fltich. The table was 13 ½ feet long and 45 inches wide. It was nothing short of exquisite. Being the gentlemen he was, Carlos pulled out her chair.

"Thank you." She blushed as he scooted her up to the table.

Carlos sat left of her.

Taking her hand, he bowed his head for grace. Surprised by his gesture and respect for God, Chyna bowed her head as well.

"Lord, I wanna say thank you for today. Thanks for this wonderful meal that I'm about to devour but most of all thank you for this beautiful creature beside me that prepared it. She's pretty special, God. I don't know what role she's going to play in my life moving forward but I thank you for her presence. I thank you for today. I thank you for her."

Chyna's heart swelled with joy. No man had ever thanked God for her. No one had ever valued her enough.

"In Jesus' name I pray; amen." Carlos lifted his head.

"That was really sweet; thank you." Chyna's cheeks burned a crimson red.

"Don't get all sappy on me. Remember you a gangsta. You ain't got no heart," he teased.

"Thugs cry," Chyna giggled.

"It's doves cry, fool." Carlos laughed.

"Whatever, let's dig in." She said dying to eat.

"Lord, please don't let me get sick," Carlos prayed.

"Shut up." Chyna pushed his arm. "Watch, you gon' be asking for seconds."

Carlos placed a forkful of rice and chicken up to his mouth and chewed. An explosion of flavor swarmed his taste buds.

"Damn, this shit good than a muthafucka." He confirmed what Chyna already knew.

"Told you." She stuck out her tongue.

"You did yo' thing, for real." He leaned over and gave her a smoldering kiss on the lips.

"Thank you." She danced around in her seat.

"You feeling better after last night?" Carlos took a bite of the asparagus.

"Yeah," Chyna shrugged.

"You know that's the second time you've called out ole boy name?"

"I know." She pushed her food around on her plate.

"'What's up wit' that?"

"It's nothing... I don't even... I don't... It's fine." Chyna tried to gather her words but found it too difficult.

She couldn't even make eye contact with him.

"It's not though and you know it," Carlos pressed the issue. "Something fucked up happened between y'all and it's fuckin' wit' yo' head. Whatever it is, you need to deal with that shit before it eats you alive."

"I'm okay." Chyna stared down at her plate.

"C'mon now. This is me you're talkin' to. You're far from okay. Look at you." He pointed at her. "The mere mention of the dude's name makes you tense as hell. What did he do to you?"

"He did a lot and so did I but I don't wanna talk about it. I just wanna enjoy my meal in peace," she stressed, feeling her temperature rise.

"Chyna, you can talk to me. I swear whatever it is I won't judge." He reached across the table to hold her hand.

"Didn't I say I didn't wanna talk about it?" She swatted his hand away. "I ain't ask you no questions about that bitch Bellamy! 'Cause guess what? I don't give a fuck about nothin' that happened between y'all. It's none of my damn business; so do us both a favor and mind your fuckin' business!" She shot up from her seat so fast she knocked over the chair.

Needing some air, Chyna stormed out onto the balcony. The sun was just starting to set. Pink and orange hues filled the afternoon sky. Chyna took a deep breath. Stressed, she placed her elbows on the railing. She never wanted to spazz out on Carlos like that. He'd been nothing short of a godsend to her but homeboy needed to learn how to leave well enough alone. There were certain lines he couldn't cross. Digging into her past was one of them.

She didn't talk about Tyreik with anyone but God. Only he understood her agony. Only God could heal her heart. For the last year and a half she'd been deeply ashamed of her behavior. She'd totally lost her sanity towards the end of their relationship. Tyreik had taken her to a place of insanity. He'd stomped on her heart so much she'd become desensitized to reality.

Any common sense she had escaped. He'd fucked her up so bad that Chyna was so afraid to fall for anyone. She never wanted to give another man the opportunity to take her back to that dark place. She was fully at peace with being alone. It felt good not to have to fight for respect, loyalty and honesty. Tyreik treated her like a stray dog off the street. He claimed to love her but the emotion he showed her was far from love.

What they shared was toxic. And although she hated the way she allowed him to treat her, Tyreik never deserved to have what happened to him. Every morning she awoke in one piece she blamed herself. She hadn't come to terms with the things that took place that day. Every time she replayed the events she wanted to lie down and die.

She wanted God to erase the memories in her head. It was so bad that sometimes she could smell the scent of his blood on her fingertips. The tormenting had to stop. Carlos would never understand the things she had to go through on a daily basis just to stay sane. Chyna wasn't happy with much outside of her daughter. She felt empty inside. Her love life was a mess and so was her career.

Chyna took another deep breath and looked out into the neighborhood. She had to calm down and make things right with Carlos. Swallowing her pride, she walked back inside. Carlos was at the table eating his food without what seemed to be a care in the world. It kind of ticked her off that he didn't come out to check on her. Chyna reclaimed her seat and placed her napkin on her lap.

"Sorry." She shot with a hint of an attitude in her voice.

"No you're not." Carlos wiped the corners of his mouth with his napkin then scooted his chair back.

Unsure of what he might do, Chyna cocked her head to the side as if to say *I wish you would.*

What happened next happened so fast it was all a blur to her. Before Chyna realized what was happening, Carlos had pushed the plates and glasses off the table and onto the floor. A thunderous crash echoed around them as Chyna's back met with the table. Carlos looked down at her frightened face. A devilish grin traced his lips. He had to let her know that her behavior would not be tolerated. He didn't know if she continued to try him 'cause he was white but Carlos was not to be fucked with. In one swoop, her booty shorts were off.

"That's yo' last time coming at me crazy. You understand?" He asked while massaging her clit.

"Yes," she whimpered, parting her legs.

"Stop playin' wit' me, Chyna." Carlos demanded as the tip of his dick slammed into her lungs.

Chyna swore she saw stars. Carlos gripped her wrists and placed them above her head with his left hand. He used his right to caress her breasts. Carlos was gripping her wrists so tight Chyna's blood circulation was starting to fade. The lack of blood running through her body only intensified her experience. Carlos could see the agony on her face but that didn't stop him from fucking the shit outta her. She had to learn a lesson.

"I'm sick of your fuckin' mouth." He grinded his hips like he was in the fight of his life. "You gon' respect me." He slapped her left titty.

"Ohhhhhhh, Carlos, fuck! You can't keep fuckin' me like this!" A tear escaped the corner of Chyna's eye.

"Oh, you want me to stop?" He paused mid-stroke.

"No! Please! No! Don't stop!" She shook her head profusely.

She desperately tried to lift her hips to fuck him back. Carlos still wouldn't budge. He loved seeing her squirm. She was dying for him to resume fucking her but Carlos wasn't going to do anything until she begged some more.

"Los, baby, please!"

"Los?" He screwed up his face. "My name is Carlos. " He slapped her thigh so she understood the repercussions of her actions.

"I'm sorry! Carlos, baby, please, fuck me! I can't take it!" She pleaded on the brink of losing her mind.

Carlos' dick was the perfect combination of pleasure and pain. The combination was lethal.

"How bad you want it?" He slid the tip in and let go of her hands.

"I want it so bad."

A stream of sticky juice trickled from the lips of her vagina.

"You do?" He allowed all ten inches of stiff rod inside her honeycomb hideout.

"Yes!" Chyna moaned, pushing his stomach back.

Carlos' dick was so big it felt like he was going to split her in half.

"Stop that shit!" He slapped her hand. "You a big girl, right?"

"Yes." Chyna whined as her eyes rolled to the back of her head.

"Then be a big girl and take this dick!" He fucked her so hard the table knocked like a bass drum.

"Now what you gon' do for this dick?" Carlos slid back out.

"Anything... you want me to suck it?" Chyna bit into her bottom lip and looked him square in the eye.

The thought of Chyna on her knees sucking him off took Carlos over the edge. Chyna held onto his back for dear life. Electricity was building in the pit of her stomach. She was about to cum.

"This pussy is mine. You understand that?" Carlos asked feeling himself about to explode.

He couldn't hold out another second longer.

"Yes!" Chyna climaxed so hard she couldn't stop repeating his name.

"Chyna!" Carlos clenched his eyes shut and climaxed.

"I love your mouth and how it feels." – Coultrain, "The Reintroduction"

#10

It was a warm 80 degrees on Memorial Day. Chyna sat in the passenger seat of Carlos' Jeep as they headed downtown. She was secretly dreading that this was her last night with him. She'd unknowingly began to enjoy his company. He got on her nerves and drove her to drink but his incredible dick game and conversation made up for his transgressions.

She couldn't front, Chyna secretly adored Carlos. He was gorgeous. She loved the way he gripped the steering wheel as his black t-shirt rippled in the wind. His black hair was slicked to the back like a 1960's bad boy. Black Ray Ban shades shielded his eyes from the blazing sun. A thin, gold chain rested against his chest. The sleeves of his t-shirt were rolled up and showcased his sleeve of tattoos. On his legs were a pair of YSL, black, fitted jeans with the knees ripped out. On his feet were a fresh pair of black, nylon, Guccissima, leather, high-top Gucci sneakers.

Chyna could stare at him until the end of time. Carlos was the first white guy she'd ever longed for. She'd only been with one other white guy in her life. Her first experience dipping into the interracial dating pond was terrible. The dude was fraudulent and his dick was the size of a pinky finger.

After that fiasco, she swore to never dip her toe back into the white boy pond but Carlos was a different story. He changed her mind about white men. Before him, she had the notion that white men were corny, weak and timid. She thought she would easily run over a white man. Carlos quickly destroyed that myth with his cockiness, brass attitude and smooth charm.

He was the truth. He didn't try to act black. He was himself. He was naturally hip and confident. She appreciated that he loved good music, black and white films and the peace and quiet of just being still. He was smart, ambitious, driven and thoughtful. If Chyna wanted a man, he would be the perfect guy.

Too bad she wasn't looking for a man. If she was, he'd be it. Falling for Carlos was a no-no. After Memorial

Day their three-day love affair would be over. Besides that, she didn't really know where he stood when it came to love. He hadn't said anything about wanting a girlfriend. For all she knew, he could still be in love with his ex.

Carlos turned onto the Landing. Hundreds of St. Louis bikers were out. Chyna watched with astonishment as guys and girls on motorcycles, motor bikes and four-wheelers whizzed by with the speed of lightning. She'd only seen things like it in Ruff Ryder videos. She never even knew that a community of bikers gathered on the Landing. The smell of burning rubber filled her nostrils as they parked.

"You ride?" She asked, eager to get out and join the party.

"Yeah." Carlos grabbed his riding gloves out of the glove compartment.

The thought of seeing him riding a motorcycle made the seat of Chyna's thong wet. Chyna switched her way around the Jeep. Carlos waited on her with his hand out. She happily smiled brightly and slipped her fingers between his. As they walked, no one could take their eyes off of them. They were stunning together. Chyna noticed a few disapproving stares from some of the brothers but gave zero fucks.

Carlos made her happy and treated her with respect. That was all that mattered to her. She could give a damn about his skin color. Plus, she was looking damn cute in one of his vintage, Queen t-shirts, Dots frayed and ripped booty shorts and $20 gladiator-style, knee-high heels. A black, lace choker and the diamond stud earrings Tyreik had bought her was the only jewelry she wore. Chyna rocked a simple red lip with no makeup. Thankfully, her skin was immaculate and even. She could get away with it. She hated when she saw girls with uneven skin rocking a bold lip. They looked like crackheads by the face.

She and Carlos maneuvered their way through the packed crowd. Everyone had their own music playing. Weed smoke filled the air. Chyna wanted in. She was dying to get blazed. Chicks gave Chyna the stink eye as she strode by on Carlos' arm. She gave each of them a look that said *be mad, bitch*! They were just jealous that she was on his arm and they weren't. She understood the hate. Carlos was every woman's wet dream come true.

"What up?" He gave dap to his pot'nahs.

"What up, my G?" Carlos' friend/employee, Fab, gave him a one-arm hug.

Fab was a short and stocky dude with a bald head.

"You bring my bike?" Carlos asked.

"Yeah, it's on the back of my truck."

"Good lookin' out." Carlos said, as his bike was brought over to him.

He had a blue, white and black Yamaha motorbike. He mounted the bike and revved the engine.

"You not gon' wear a helmet?" Chyna asked concerned for his safety.

"Nah, baby girl. I'm good." He grinned at her naivety. "Let me get warmed up and I'ma take you for a ride." He announced as her phone rang.

Chyna checked to make sure it wasn't India. It wasn't. It was another private call. Chyna quickly hit ignore and focused back on Carlos. She didn't feel like cussing a bitch out on a national holiday.

"I'm not gettin' on that thing. I got a child to live for." Chyna rolled her neck.

"You got a what?" Carlos said surprised.

"I have a daughter." She repeated like he was dumb.

"Since when?"

"Since 1999," she laughed.

"Where is your daughter?" Carlos side-eyed her.

"Don't look at me like that. I ain't no deadbeat mama. My daughter is 15 years old and she's backpacking through Europe for the summer with her school."

"Oh, a'ight, 'cause I was gettin' ready to call DFS on yo' ass," Carlos said seriously.

"Whatever, does me having a child bother you?" She quizzed, praying to God it didn't.

"No, it just never came up in conversation. You never told me that."

"I thought I did but maybe I didn't because I have no intention on seeing you after today." She said feeling the sting of her words as they slipped off her tongue.

She knew she was being cruel but she had to remind herself that catching feelings for Carlos was not an option.

"You don't know what God has in store for me and you." He winked his eye and placed on his gloves.

Carlos tried to act like her words didn't affect him but they did.

"Jesus knows my heart. This shit is a wrap after today, honey," Chyna cackled.

"Yeah a'ight. That's what yo' mouth say." Carlos revved up the engine again and took off.

Chyna watched on pins and needles as he popped a wheelie while doing almost 75 miles an hour. She had never been so nervous for anyone in her life. She didn't like to see Carlos zooming down the street amongst the other bikers doing stunts and tricks. Someone could get really hurt. All of the commotion reminded her of the car crash Tyreik had. It was all too much. Chyna was experiencing sensory overload.

"What's up, future baby mama?" She heard a voice say from behind.

Chyna looked over her shoulder and found L.A. coming her way. She had to make sure her mouth was closed so she wouldn't start drooling. L.A. sipped on a bottle of Jack as he neared. His hair was freshly cut. The waves in his head were spinning. His shiny, black beard called her name. He wore no shirt. L.A.'s sculpted biceps and six-pack were on full display. He was 180 pounds of caramel wonder. A tattoo of a cross stretched across his pecks with the words dedication and loyalty tattooed above.

A pair of Dsquared2, bleached, paint splatter jeans hung low off his waist. His Calvin Klein boxers kissed the happy trail of hair leading down to his dick. *Blue Ivy, be a hedge of protection,* Chyna prayed. *Please don't let me fuck this man.*

"You tried it." She turned around and looked him up-and-down with a displeased expression on her face.

"You know you happy to see me." He stepped into her personal space and wrapped her up in his embrace.

The scent of his John Varvatos cologne was too much for Chyna to handle. A fine man wearing great smelling cologne was one of her weaknesses.

"You miss me?" He whispered into her ear.

His warm breath tickled her ear. *This nigga crazy,* Chyna thought as she felt his dick press up against her stomach. *And it's big. Fuck, I'ma suck it.*

"You need to back the hell up off me." She pushed him away afraid that Carlos would see.

"Don't act like you ain't enjoy it. You liked it," L.A. grinned.

"No, I didn't," Chyna lied, ashamed that she did.

"Where my boy at?" He surveyed the crowd.

"On his bike. He'll be right back so you need to chill with your li'l stunts." Chyna shot him an evil glare.

"So what's up wit' y'all?" L.A. ignored her warning.

"What you mean?" Chyna cocked her head to the side and folded her arms across her chest.

"Y'all together?"

"You nosey." Chyna tuned up her face.

"Nah, I'm interested." L.A. looked her up-and-down lustfully.

"In what?" She arched her brow.

"In you," L.A. clarified.

Chyna's heart skipped a beat. L.A. was really trying her edges with all of his slick, one-liners. Just when she was about to hit him with a slick, one-liner of her own and tell him she wasn't interested, Carlos rode up on his bike. He straddled the bike and took off his gloves. The look he was giving Chyna let her know that he wasn't pleased with her having a side conversation with L.A.

"Come here." He said in a low, commanding tone.

Like water for chocolate, Chyna floated over to him. No matter whom she found intriguing or attractive, Carlos had complete control over her body. Chyna stood before him nervously. She couldn't believe she cared if he knew she was misbehaving. She hated the way he affected her. Carlos stared deep into her big brown eyes. He could see the fear that lie behind her brown irises. He didn't want her to fear him. He just wanted her to respect him at all times.

"You ready to ride?" He asked, caressing her dimpled cheek softly.

"I'm scared," Chyna replied, lost in his touch.

"I got you. You know I'ma keep you safe." He pulled her into him by the back of her neck.

Carlos kissed her luscious lips with so much intensity Chyna's legs went limp. Each time their lips met she was exported into outer space. Carlos knew exactly how to reel her in every time. The sexual chemistry they shared couldn't be matched. Carlos gave her one last peck on the lips then released her from his grasp. Chyna had to steady her balance so she wouldn't fall. Now that he'd marked his territory, Carlos acknowledged L.A.'s presence. If L.A. didn't know that Chyna was his, he knew now.

"What up?" He gave him a five.

"What up?" L.A. slapped the palm of his hand.

"How long you been here?"

"For a minute. I got in a couple of runs." L.A. wiped his forehead with a towel. "I see you brought miss lady wit' you. Y'all gettin' serious?"

"No, we're just friends," Chyna spoke up.

Carlos narrowed his eyes at her. He wanted to slap the shit outta her. Yeah, they were just friends but she didn't have to volunteer that information to L.A. It made Carlos wonder if she was feeling L.A. on the low. He and Chyna weren't officially together but he'd staked his claim on her. She needed to chill wit' all the extra-friendly shit. Pissed, he snatched the bottle of Jack from L.A.'s hand and took a long swig.

He had to chill before he blacked out on Chyna and L.A. She had no idea the type of games L.A. liked to play. Since high school they'd been in competition with each other. They were both beast on the basketball court. Each of them got into Duke for college basketball but due to a knee injury, Carlos had to forgo his scholarship.

L.A. went on to dominate college basketball. He even got a contract to play for the Los Angeles Lakers. Carlos envied the fact that L.A. got to live out his dream of playing professional basketball. He'd done well with his slew of successful businesses but his heart remained on the court.

L.A. may have gotten his dream career but Carlos got the dream girl. Him, L.A. and Bellamy all went to the same high school. She was the most beautiful, smart and popular girl in their graduating class. Bellamy could have any boy she wanted. Many dudes, including Carlos and L.A., pined after her but she wanted Carlos. L.A. didn't understand what she saw in him. His family was dirt poor immigrants.

He didn't rock the latest fashions or high-priced sneakers. He didn't even have a car during high school. He rode the bus but Bellamy saw past all of that. She saw potential in Carlos. She knew he was a diamond in the rough. All she had to do was give him guidance and lead him the right way. Carlos was tough and strong. He didn't take any of her shit. He was the perfect guy for her.

L.A. couldn't stand that he'd lost out on being with Bellamy. It really got under his skin that he lost out to Carlos. In his eyes, Carlos wasn't on his level. He was an a'ight looking white boy that came from nothing. Carlos didn't have L.A.'s family lineages. He came from a good, upper-class family. He wasn't used to not getting what he wanted. He and Carlos would never be best friends. They would always be frenemies.

"Oh word? Y'all just friends? Well come take a ride wit' me then!" L.A. gestured for her to get on the back of his bike.

"She good." Carlos responded for her.

Chyna bucked her eyes and tried her hardest not to laugh. Carlos and L.A. were ridiculous. Both men needed to grow up.

"Umm, I can speak for myself." She put her dick out on the table.

"Yeah, dog, chill out," L.A. agreed. "Let li'l mama speak for herself."

"Get on," Carlos signaled to Chyna to get on his bike.

He didn't give a fuck what they were talking about.

"You really need to work on your social skills," L.A. joked.

"Social skills these nuts." Carlos handed Chyna a helmet.

"Yeah, a'ight." L.A. sucked his teeth.

Carlos could try to keep Chyna away from him all he wanted. It didn't matter. He'd eventually get some time alone with her. It was only a matter of time before she learned the truth about the man she was falling for.

The moon smiled down upon Carlos as he did 70 on the highway. After riding bikes for hours with his people and nearly giving Chyna a heart attack, he took her out to a well-deserved dinner at Sub Zero Vodka Bar. Sub Zero was located in the Central West End. They served over 500 different types of vodka and some of the best sushi St. Louis had to offer. They even had an ice bar.

Sub Zero was one of Chyna's favorite restaurants. She was pleased to learn it was one of Carlos' favorites too. Full off of sashimi and tempura vegetables, they coasted along Highway 40. The sky was filled with stars. Wind gusted over their body as they vibed out to Coultrain's *Kiss of Death*. Coultrain was one of St. Louis' most underrated artist. He had a voice that marveled Nat King Cole and lyrics that would leave you paralyzed.

His latest EP, *The Side Effects of Make Believe Divided for Love Sake*, was on her best albums of 2015 list. Chyna loved riding through the city at night. When things were good between them, she and Tyreik would hop in his car and ride around for hours with nowhere in particular to go. They'd listen to music and get lost in the scenery and their thoughts.

Chyna looked over at Carlos as he drove. *How am I going to say goodbye to him tomorrow,* she wondered rubbing the back of his head. In such a short amount of time he'd quietly become a part of her. It was comforting to know she wouldn't have to wake up alone. The presence of his company had become a crutch for her. She needed to stay near him. He enveloped her. He was what her body craved.

Chyna knew what she was about to do was dangerous and crazy but she needed him to fill her up with his thick rod. Slowly, she slid her hand down his chest. He delighted in her touch. Carlos held his breath as she unzipped his jeans. He didn't say a word as she pulled out his erect dick. Chyna eased out of her shorts and crawled over into the driver's seat. Straddling his lap, she placed a trail of kisses from his cheek down to his neck.

"What you doing?" Carlos gazed over her shoulder so he could see the road.

"Saying thank you." She licked and sucked his earlobe.

"For what?" Carlos tried his hardest to concentrate on the road.

"For this weekend." She grinded her hips.

She could feel his breathing increase with each flicker of her tongue. Using her right hand, she eased her way down onto his eagerly awaiting dick. Carlos filled very inch of her up. Chyna wound her hips to a slow, sensual pace. She wanted him to feel every bit of friction they were creating.

"I'm gonna miss you." She sat up straight and looked him square in the eye.

Carlos took his eyes off the road and studied her face. He wanted to tell her he'd miss her too but his mouth wouldn't form the words. He'd already fallen down the rabbit hole. He couldn't lose any more of himself in her. Instead, he took his hands off the steering wheel and wrapped her up in his embrace.

Carlos guided the wheel with his knee as they ravished each other. He never experienced something so heavenly and sinful. He could forget about the world when he was with her. Chyna was too hot to handle. He began to wonder if he'd ever be able to tame her. Her warm breath on his neck tickled his soul. The soft flesh of her inner thigh consumed him to the point he thought he might crash. He desperately wanted to steal a kiss from her forbidden lips. The rush of the night air on their skin made them both shudder and moan.

Each deep thrust into his shaft caused Chyna to quack. She would never be satisfied with just 72 hours of him. Carlos was the type of man it would take a lifetime to consume. She needed him inside her forever. He was embedded in her D.N.A. He could drown her in his semen and she'd gladly swallow every drop. The insatiable lust she had for him was unfathomable. It seemed impossible but she had to figure out a way to let him go.

"Why you caught up in your feelings?" – Keke Palmer, I "Don't Belong To You"

#11

Rays of sunlight escaped through the blinds as Carlos lie on top of Chyna. Her right leg was hiked up in the air as his tongue slid up her thigh. His diamond chain and Audemars Piguet watch sparkled under the sunshine. Chyna ran her hand over the tattoos on his arm. Her lips wanted to kiss each of them goodbye but her brain knew better. She was a woman of her word. Once she left his crib there would be no communication.

She didn't even know if his number was still the same and she for damn sure wasn't going to ask. This was the end. He was going to go his way and she'd go hers. Sure, she'd miss the hell out of him but this is where they parted ways. There was no room or space in her life for fairytales and romance. Behind romance always lies pain.

The last time she gave her heart to a man, her heart and his burned into flames. Love beat Chyna black and blue. It had never been good to her. No matter how much she secretly wanted to keep her and Carlos' weekend love affair going, logic won out. She had to let him go.

Carlos gazed into Chyna's eyes with a yearning inside his heart he'd never felt before. She hadn't even left yet and he already missed her. He'd unknowingly gotten used to her sassiness, quick temper, laughter, moans of ecstasy and Cover Girl smile. She fit perfectly in his arms when they slept. He didn't know what he'd do when he turned over at night and she wasn't there.

Yeah, she was fucked up, but so was he. They were both two fucked up puzzle pieces that fit perfectly together. Carlos knew a future with her wasn't in the cards. With the mind frame he was in, he'd potentially destroy her. Chyna was a tough girl but he knew she was really made of cotton candy and rainbows. She was dying to be loved and accepted but he could never give her what she wanted. His heart was closed for good. He dug her a lot and wanted to keep her around so he could delight in her wonder but that's all it could ever be.

He would love to have her in his life without a title of commitment but women couldn't detach their heart from sex and kicking it. Chyna played tough but she was no different. And no, he didn't want to see her with anyone else but that was a chance he was willing to take. Chyna palmed his face with her hands.

"You gon' miss me?" She couldn't help but ask.

It hadn't slipped past her that he hadn't said he would.

"Why? You gon' miss me?" He flipped the script on her.

"I already said I was." She wrapped her legs around his back and pulled him in closer.

Instead of answering, Carlos placed loving kisses all over her collarbone. He hoped she wouldn't press the issue and just be cool. It was already hard accepting the fact that he would be dropping her off soon. Chyna could see the hesitation in his eyes. *Ok, don't answer me,* she thought somewhat hurt. It was obvious that their weekend together hadn't affected him like it had her. Chyna would never let Carlos know that her heart had been punctured by him. She was going to keep it cute and put her poker face on. She would not play herself and act like a girl about it. If he wanted to keep it casual, she had no problem playing that game too.

"I'ma miss this." He sensually kissed the exposed flesh of her breasts that stuck out of her bra. "And this..." He slid down and kissed her stomach.

"And most definitely this." He kissed the face of her pussy causing her to convulse.

Carlos still hadn't gone down on her. Chyna honestly didn't know if she'd be able to handle it if he did.

"You're not playing fair." She gasped for air.

"I never do." He grinned easing his way back up. "What time your landlord say you can pick up the key?" Carlos asked resting on his back.

In one swift motion, Chyna was now lying on his chest.

"Twelve."

Carlos checked his watch. It was 10:30a.m. He had a short amount of time left with her.

"How long you been living there?"

"Ooooh… umm, almost six years. Me and my ex got the place together but it's mine now." Chyna spoke almost above a whisper.

Memories of the day she and Tyreik sat with the landlord at Soulard Coffee Garden signing the renter's agreement popped in her mind. Moving to the Southside of St. Louis was supposed to help their relationship. Things, however, only got worse.

"Sometimes I think about moving because of all the bad memories and war stories we had in that house but I love my place so much it's hard to let go."

"It seems like it's hard for you to let him go too." Carlos pointed out hoping she would open up.

"It's not that I can't let him go. I've already done that. I can't get past what happened. That's the hard part." Chyna put her head down.

"What happened?" Carlos used his index finger to lift her head up.

A raincloud of sorrow washed over Chyna as tears filled the brim of her eyes.

"Our relationship was always on 100. Me and him fought all the time, so fighting for me became a normal thing. Each time we got into it we both found ways to up the ante." She tried to catch her breath. "The last time we fought I took things too far." She swallowed hard.

"What you do?" Carlos wrinkled his forehead mad curious. "You ain't kill him did you?" He eyed her suspiciously.

"Almost." She blinked profusely as tears dripped down her face.

Chyna couldn't believe she was actually about to reveal her deep, dark secret to him. She never talked about Tyreik to anyone, not even her girls. The weight of that day was unbearable. She couldn't escape it. She had to talk about it to gain some clarity. Plus, it didn't matter if she told Carlos. She wouldn't see him again, so it didn't matter what he would think of her after he knew.

"He was in his car trying to leave and I was being a crazy, psychotic bitch. I wouldn't let him go. I was so hurt I just wanted him to see what he'd done to me. So I kept banging on the hood of his car yelling at him to stay and talk to me. But he just kept on ignoring me and I felt so insignificant and small. I felt invisible. He was so in a rush to get away from me that he didn't pay attention as he backed out of the driveway." Chyna bit her bottom lip and willed herself not to pass out.

She was so lost in the story she'd forgotten Carlos was there.

"I saw the school bus coming. I tried to scream but it wouldn't come out. It was too late." She broke down and cried. "Before I knew it, the car had flipped over. I tried to get him out. I tried so hard," she sobbed.

"But he was trapped inside." Her bottom lip quivered. "Blood was everywhere. He was barely conscious. His breathing was short and I felt so helpless. He took his last breath right in front of me."

"Damn," Carlos uttered, bugged out. "I thought you said he didn't die?"

"No-no-no, he didn't." Chyna came back to reality. "Thankfully, the ambulance arrived and the EMT's revived him but for weeks he was on life support. We all thought he was going to die. He had several strokes while he was unconscious. When he finally came to, his memory was sparse. He had to relearn how to walk and talk. I wanted to be there to help him during his rehabilitation but he didn't want to have anything to do with me." Chyna looked at Carlos so he could see how devastated she was.

"He hated my guts and blamed me for the accident. I didn't blame him for being angry. I blamed me too. It was all my fault. I should've just let him go but I just had to have the last word. I almost killed him. Every day that I wake up healthy and mobile with no problems makes me feel sick inside. I don't know how he's doing now 'cause he won't talk to me, so I don't know if he's made a full recovery or not. He's completely etched me out of his life. I wish I could shake the guilt but I can't. It consumes me. It follows me wherever I go." She wept uncontrollably.

Chyna wanted to run and hide from her emotions but she was stuck.

"Shhhh, baby doll," Carlos rested her head on his chest and consoled her.

His chest was soaked with her tears.

"It's ok. It wasn't your fault," he whispered.

"Yes it is," Chyna sobbed. "He almost died because of me." She cried so hard the angels up above heard her cries.

"You can't continue to blame yourself. You have to forgive yourself for your part in the argument and move on. He's alive. You didn't kill him."

"I know but I almost did." Chyna wiped her face.

She hated being vulnerable.

"The last I heard he was still in rehab. I don't know who's taking care of him. He has no family. I was his family so I don't know who's holding him down and making sure he's straight."

"No news is good news, right?" Carlos said trying to make her feel better.

"I don't know." She shrugged sitting Indian style. "I can't believe this is me right now. I don't cry. This ain't me. Why the fuck am I crying? I feel like a straight pussy."

"You can't be tough all the time, Chy. You gotta let somebody in sometime."

"Lies you tell. When you let people in you get hurt. I've been hurt enough. Tyreik is the reason I don't want to be in a relationship now. He broke me down. I never want to go through that shit ever again. He made me feel like I was worthless. I feel bad for how things went down between us but I would never be back with that nigga or anybody else for that matter. I'm good on that love shit. Fuck letting somebody in." She swallowed her tears and bossed up.

"You gon' get enough of that tough shit. It's gon' fuck you up one day," Carlos warned. "I know we won't be rockin' wit' each other after today but I wanna see you happy. You deserve it." He ran his thumb back and forth across her cheek.

"Thank you. I'ma be alright though. I got my daughter and my weed so I'll be straight," she joked.

"Yeah a'ight," he chuckled. "I know this is off the subject but uh…. what were you and L.A. talkin' about yesterday when I rode up?" Carlos quizzed.

Chyna looked around confused for a second. She didn't know why Carlos was bringing L.A.'s name up.

"Uhhhh, nothing," she replied caught off guard by his line of questioning. "But yo, nah, hold up." She situated herself. "What's going on wit' y'all? What is this li'l rivalry y'all got going on? It's weird."

"We straight. I ain't got no problem with that man. I just know how he move. I know he like you."

"How you figure that?" Chyna drew her head back.

"'Cause I can tell. He looks at you the same way I do," Carlos confessed.

"So basically you're sayin' you're in love with me?" Chyna teased.

"Not at all."

"No, you like me!" Chyna urged him to admit it.

"This ain't about me," Carlos smirked.

"You like me." She smiled, happy.

"Whatever." Carlos waved her off.

"You *liiiiiiiike* me." She tickled the side of his stomach.

"Stop!" Carlos laughed pushing her hand away.

"But nah, for real. So what if L.A. like me. Why does it bother you? You agreed that us seeing each other past today wouldn't be a good idea. I mean...unless you've changed your mind," she probed, hoping he had.

"I haven't." Carlos shook his head

Chyna's stomach dropped from disappointment but her face remained stoned.

"Ok, so if L.A. is digging me that shouldn't affect you and if I like him that shouldn't move you either, right?"

"So you saying you like him?" Carlos screwed up his face, heated.

"No, but if I did you shouldn't care." Chyna persisted knowing she was hitting a nerve. "You don't like me so it shouldn't matter."

"Yeah, a'ight." Carlos rolled off the bed pissed. "If you wanna fuck wit' him, fuck wit' him. I don't care. We grown. You can do what you wanna do."

"Damn, it's like that?" Chyna said appalled by his reaction.

"Yeah, as far as I'm concerned, this weekend never happened."

"That's really how you feel?" She questioned visibly hurt.

"You ready to go? I don't want you to miss yo' landlord," he replied, throwing a t-shirt on over his head.

"Chile, please, let me get my stuff ready then," Chyna sneered, heated.

"Yeah, you do that."

"She Instagram herself like bad bitch alert." – Kanye West, "Blood On The Leaves"

#12

Chyna sat in the back of an Uber staring out of the window. It was a perfect Saturday afternoon. There wasn't a cloud in sight. The sun was out. It was a blazing 90 degrees. Visions of Carlos flashed before her eyes. She hadn't been able to get him out of her mind. She found herself daydreaming of lying in his arms. Sleeping alone was a punishment she didn't want to partake in anymore. She'd become accustomed to the intoxicating smell of his cologne and how it seeped into her skin.

Chyna hadn't even bothered washing one of the shirts she wore during the time they spent together. She'd find herself pulling it out and inhaling the scent just so she could feel like he was around. She'd willingly take the blame for the way they left things if that meant she could be back in his presence. She would've loved to be spending her day with him. But Carlos wasn't fucking with her. It had been four days since she had seen or heard from him.

After the way they left things, she wasn't really sure if she ever wanted to see him again. He was a complete dickhead to her. Sure she'd had her bitchy moments and sort of egged the argument on, but he didn't have to be so cold-hearted towards her. She thought they'd made progress. Especially after she'd opened up to him about Tyreik, but when he dropped her off at home he didn't even bother to say goodbye.

Chyna sat there for a minute like a dummy waiting for some form of acknowledgement of her presence but he had nothing but contempt for her. He stared straight ahead and acted as if she wasn't even there. Chyna was crushed. She never expected Carlos to be so childish and cruel. He never got into his feelings. Apparently a Chyna and L.A. pairing posed a huge threat to him. Chyna was beyond confused 'cause he acted like he didn't want her.

He never clarified his feelings towards her. He avoided the conversation like the plague. It didn't really bother Chyna because being together wasn't an option for either of them. So there shouldn't have been a problem. Situations like this were exactly why Chyna played the field and kept her feelings close to her chest. Caring for someone was an absolute nuisance. *Fuck Carlos,* she tried to convince herself as the Uber dropped her off. Chyna sauntered into Peacemaker Lobster and Crab Co. and looked around for her friends.

Peacemaker Lobster and Crab was a fairly new restaurant that was gaining momentum. Chef Kevin Nasham followed the path of Acadians from Canada through Maine and New Orleans to Lafayette, Louisiana to create his menu. Chyna was a huge seafood lover so she couldn't wait to dive in. Spotting her crew, she sashayed across the restaurant. Dressed to kill, she drew attention from the other patrons.

Chyna loved that she turned heads when she entered a room. She never left the house without being put together. She loved being girly and feminine. She loved flexing on bitches. Instead of flat ironing her short hair, she let her short curls flow wildly. The ringlet curls framed her heart-shaped face perfectly.

Chyna's beat of the day was soft and sultry. Her skin was bronzed to perfection. To top off the beat she wore a bold, chocolate brown, matte lip. Her look consisted of her diamond stud earrings, a gold choker, white sports bra-inspired top, grey joggers and a grey, lightweight sweater which was tied around her waist. Gold cuffs adorned each of her ankles. Her favorite, black, Louboutin "Pigalle", six inch heels gave her the added height she so desperately needed.

She had a sexy, sporty, athletic look going on. Her tight and toned abs were on full display. She looked damn good and felt like a million bucks. The buzz she had from her morning solo smoke session had her in a great mood. Nothing was going to fuck up her day. Her other best friends, Asia and Jaylen, and their beautiful 2 and a half year-old son, Aiden, were in town for two weeks.

Chyna only got to see her friends every few months so anytime she spent with them was a blessing. She was meeting them and Brooke for lunch so they could catch up and talk shit. Checking up on her friends was important to her. Chyna didn't like a lot of people. She only fucked wit' a select few and Brooke, Asia and Jaylen were her day 1 hittas.

"Ok, Hollywood," Asia snapped her finger as Chyna neared the table. "You look cute, bitch."

"Thanks, boo." Chyna gleamed curtseying.

Asia looked equally as good. To Chyna, Asia was the prettiest woman she'd ever seen. The girl was stunning. She was Asian and black so she had that exotic thing going for her. Men lost their minds over her. Jaylen constantly had to check niggas over his wife. She was short and petite like Chyna but her hair was so long it touched her butt. Jaylen wasn't too bad looking himself. He was super tall, caramel with a low-cut. He played for the Chicago Bulls and had just re-signed for a cool 100 mill.

"I hate you," Brooke laughed.

"You just mad that my outfit look better than yours." Chyna playfully pushed her in the arm. "Let me kiss my god-baby." She raced over to Aiden and picked him up.

He'd grown an inch since the last time she'd seen him. Chyna inhaled his sweet baby scent and melted. She loved Aiden so much. She held him tight and kissed his chubby cheeks.

"Put my baby down smelling like weed smoke," Jaylen frowned.

"Let me find out you a hater. You just mad 'cause you can't have none."

"I actually am," Jaylen laughed.

"I missed my baby." Chyna kissed Aiden once more then sat him back in the highchair.

"Don't think I was gon' let it slip. You're late, ho," Asia rolled her eyes.

"I'm sorry, friend." Chyna gave her a hug.

"I know you are." Asia hugged her back.

She was genuinely happy to see her sister/friend. After everything that had happened to Chyna over the last year and a half, Asia constantly worried that her friend was on the brink of a meltdown.

"Come on, let's take an usie." Chyna pulled out her iPhone.

She and Asia posed for the flick like they were Beyoncé. To be as expected, the picture was cute. Chyna posted it on Instagram with the caption: **Bad Bitch Alert** and the location of the restaurant.

"What up, big head?" She gave Jaylen a five.

"You got nerve," he chuckled.

"I know you're happy the season is over for y'all." Chyna sat down.

"I am."

"Can I get you something to drink?" The waitress asked Chyna.

"Yes please; can I have a glass of red wine? Whatever kind you have will be fine."

"Sure, I'll be right back." The waitress walked away.

"What is up wit yo' boy Derek Rose? That nigga always hurt. Has he ever finished a season without ending up on the injured list?" Chyna continued her conversation with Jaylen.

"That's 'cause he light skin," Brooke chimed in.

Everybody cracked up laughing.

"Yo, I'm starting to think he Samuel L. Jackson in Unbreakable," Jaylen joked.

"So how was y'all holiday weekend?" Asia asked. "We had a ball in the Hamptons."

"Don't nobody care." Chyna spat sarcastically.

"We asked yo' dumb-ass if you wanted to go two months ago and you said you didn't know."

"I didn't," Chyna pouted as the waitress placed her glass of wine before her. "I have a kid and a household to take care of. I just can't be running off to the Hamptons like it's nothing. Plus, I had to pay for India's trip to Europe. A bitch gotta save her coins. It's been hard not having Tyreik around."

"Shit, you was struggling when he was around," Brooke reminded her.

"Really, bitch? Really?" Chyna glared at her. "You really gon' go there?"

"I'm just saying." Brooke bucked her eyes and sipped on her drink.

"Please don't make me slap you 'cause I'm mad at you too."

"What I do?" Brooke placed her hand on her chest, apalled.

"You left me too, heffa."

"Umm, excuse you. I had dick waiting on me in L.A. I wasn't gon' pass that up to run around St. Louis with you all weekend."

Chyna groaned and rolled her eyes.

"Don't even bring up the word L.A."

"Why?" Asia asked as they all looked over the menu.

"Ooooh… my bad." Brooke giggled knowing the tea.

"What?" Asia died to know.

She hated being out of the loop.

"Before I tell you, let's order 'cause a bitch got the munchies and need to eat." Chyna said as the waitress came back over to take their orders.

Once the menus were cleared she inhaled deeply and popped her lips. Asia was on the edge of her seat awaiting the news.

"So, I spent the holiday weekend locked out of my house."

"How in the hell did you do that, Chyna?" Asia replied. "I told you to lay off the weed and pills."

"Ummmm, excuse you, Iyanla. I wasn't high when I lost my keys. Well, I was a little loaded but that's not the point," Chyna waved her off. "My keys fell out my purse after I hit this dude that look like he stay on the Northside of St. Louis wit' my clutch."

"Who are you?" Jaylen eyed her quizzically.

Her life was a mess.

"I'm Chyna Danea Black and don't you forget it." She laughed hitting him with the middle finger. "Y'all, I ain't have no money, no nothing."

"So where did you stay all weekend? Did you go over your mama house?" Asia asked.

"Hell naw, staying with Diane didn't even cross my mind," Chyna shook her head.

"Nah, she stayed with her boo thang," Brooke grinned, wickedly.

"Boo thang? Chyna don't like nobody," Asia said in disbelief.

"Yes she does. Asia, you remember that dude she met a while back name Carlos?" Brooke questioned.

"Aww yeah, Carlos. He could get it. He was a fine li'l white boy." Asia fanned herself with her hand.

"Chill," Jaylen warned.

"I'm sorry, baby." She rubbed his hand.

"Say he fine again," Jaylen put a butter knife up to her throat. "I'll kill ya." He imitated Ike Turner.

"I-I-I-I- I sorry, Ike." Asia played along.

"Y'all are ridiculous," Chyna laughed, enjoying their banter.

"You little mad or big mad?" Asia winked her eye at Chyna then flicked her tongue against Jaylen's tongue.

"I'ma throw up my food before it even get here." Chyna pretended to earl.

"Now back to the story." Asia rubbed her hands together giddily. "How was your weekend with him? Did y'all..." She popped her booty in her seat simulating sex.

"What's my name?" Chyna looked at her like she was dumb. "Duh."

"Was it good?" Asia mouthed.

"Magically delicious. The best dick I've ever had." Chyna closed her eyes and reminisced.

"Really?" Asia replied shocked.

"She got her some good ole vitamin D." Brooke smacked her lips.

"I'm gettin' ready to go," Jaylen scooted back his chair.

"Ok, babe, we'll stop talkin' about it." Asia pulled him back up to the table just as their food arrived.

"Can I have some more wine please," Chyna held up her glass.

"Sure." The waitress filled her glass to the center.

"Are you going to see him again?" Asia questioned chewing her food.

"No." Chyna shook her head.

"She's fuckin' insane." Brooke spoke up.

"Listen," Chyna put down her fork. "Carlos is a great guy. I had fun with him but he's just as fucked up as I am. We will kill each other."

"Ugh, is he another Tyreik?" Asia frowned, disappointed.

"No, he's not that bad but the man does have more issues than Vogue." She picked up her fork and played with her food. "Then he has this ex-girlfriend that I'm not sure he's over and this weird rivalry with his homeboy who likes me. Who's name, by the way, is L.A. It's just way too much."

Chyna sighed. She missed Carlos tremendously. She wanted to see him or at least hear his voice. But she had to suck it up and remember that liking him was no bueno.

"OMG, you like him," Asia gushed.

"What?" Chyna came back to reality.

"You like him. It's written all over your face."

"He a'ight." Chyna played it off.

"Mmm hmm... I bet he is." Asia twisted her lips to the side.

"I'm done talking about this. Y'all ruining my fuckin' meal." Chyna bit into her Lobster Po'boy sandwich. "Oh my God. This is fuckin' delicious." She closed her eyes and relished the taste of the sweet lobster and tangy aioli sauce.

The next thing she knew, a warm splash of wine hit her face.

"What the fuck?" She screeched.

To her surprise, when she popped open her eyes she found some Sofia Vergara lookin' bitch standing over her. The chick was drop-dead gorgeous. She had long, thick, brown hair with blonde highlights. She had diamond-shaped brown eyes, a button nose and pearly white teeth. The chick was serving the restaurant body in a body hugging, olive green, tank dress. The girl was shaped like Jessica Rabbit. If Chyna was into women and didn't have plans on beating her ass, she would've got on her.

"I no jur fuckin' my hussss-band." The Latina woman yelled.

Everyone in the restaurant turned to watch the commotion.

"Chyna, you know this ho?" Brooke asked ready to pop-off.

Chyna was so caught off guard it took her a minute to speak. Her eyes were burning and more importantly, her outfit was ruined. Red wine was all over her top and joggers.

"Nah, I don't know this crazy bitch! Who are you?" She wiped her eyes with her hands.

"I told ju already; my name is Selena." Selena folded her arms across her chest and stood back on one leg. "I've *been* callin' jur phone. I no jur fuckin' my hussss-band."

"Bitch, I don't know your *huuuuusband*!" Chyna mocked her. "Who is yo' nigga?" She blinked profusely.

"Waymon, ju were *wiiiith* hem last night. I no ju were 'cause he didn't come home last night." Selena yelled causing her thick Spanish accent to shine through.

"Chyna, were you with this girl husband last night?" Asia stressed nervously.

"Really?" Chyna shot Asia a stern look.

"I mean, we know how you get down." Asia held up her hands in defense.

"No, I didn't even go out last night." Chyna grimaced then turned her attention back on Selena. "And, bitch, I don't know no nigga name Waymon!"

"Oh *veally,* then why is jur name and jur number in my man's phone?"

"I don't know!" Chyna shrilled. "I fucks mad niggas. I get around! Who knows how yo' nigga got my number! What you need to be concerned with is me rag taggin' that ass!" Chyna hopped out of her seat.

"So ju don't no my husss-band?" Selena jumped back and covered her face.

"Bitch! Are you deaf; I said no!"

"Ju don't know hem?" Selena held her phone up so Chyna could see a pic of Waymon.

Chyna quickly recognized the dude's face. He was the dude she banged on the fire escape outside of Mandarin. She had totally forgotten about him.

"Aww shit, that's him," she groaned, slapping her hand against her thigh.

"Jes." Selena pressed her lips together knowing she was right.

"Oh my bad. I did fuck him," Chyna confessed, exasperated.

"Chyna!" Asia gasped.

"What? I didn't know he was married" Chyna shrugged.

"Ahhhhhhh-ha-ahhhhhhhhh," Selena wailed. "I knew it! I knew ju were slipping with my hussss-band!"

"Can you say it any louder?" Chyna looked around at all the starring faces, embarrassed.

"Jur slipping with my hussss-band! JUR SLIPPING WITH MY HUSSSS-BAND!" Selena sobbed as she fell out on the floor.

"You really need to calm down," Chyna insisted trying to quiet her down.

"Ju don't tell me to calm down. Homeworker!" Selena stood up and grabbed Brooke's drink.

Before Chyna knew it, she'd splashed her in the face again.

This time a rush of ice-cold Sprite ran down her face and chest.

"Oh hell naw! Bitch, you about to die!" Chyna charged towards her only to be stopped by Jaylen. "Uh ah,

Jaylen! Let me go!" She swung her arms, trying to break loose.

"Ju better not touch me! I have 911 on sped dial," Selena warned.

Chyna thought of her daughter and stopped trying to break free from Jaylen's hold. She couldn't risk going to jail over a scorned wife.

"Look, girl, when I met your husband, I didn't know he was married. He didn't even have a ring on. We smashed and that was it. I haven't talked to him since. The only reason I gave him my number is because he kept beggin' for it."

"Veally?" Tears slid down Selena's solemn face.

For a second, Chyna felt sorry for her. Then she remembered that her outfit was ruined. Chyna immediately saw red again.

"I put that on my daughter, you crazy bitch," she said truthfully.

"Ju swear ju weren't wit' hem last night?" Selena asked skeptical.

"I already told you no, girl," Chyna said fed up with being questioned.

"So if he wasn't wit' ju, who was he wit' then?" Selena said to herself.

"I don't know, girl, and I don't care. I will tell you this though." Chyna pushed Jaylen's hands away. "The next time you think about running up on a bitch and throwing drinks, make sure you got the right bitch! Shit like that will get you killed!" Chyna wiped her top and joggers off with a napkin.

"I'm sorry," Selena cried.

"Uh ah, sorry my ass. How did you know where to find me?" Chyna died to know.

"Ju posted a pic on... how do ju say... Insta-ram. Ju put jur location. That's how I found ju," Selena sniffled.

"Social media will get you fucked up for real," Brooke slurped through a straw what was left in her glass. "That's a damn shame,'" she shook her head. "Can I get another Sprite, please?"

"I just want you to want me the way that I want you and more." – Jazmine Sullivan, "Let It Burn"

#13

Art, Beats + Lyrics was an annual event that hit St. Louis once a year. It was a traveling art and music tour presented by Jack Daniel's Tennessee Honey and Gentleman Jack. The tour visited Houston, New Orleans, St. Louis and Birmingham. It was a free event that drew hundreds of people. That year, Mystikal was on the bill to perform. Over 50 visual artist and photographers would be represented. It would be Chyna's first time attending.

She was hella excited. All of St. Louis would be there. She was even more excited that she'd be going with Asia, Jaylen and Brooke. After the fiasco at the restaurant with Selena, she was in desperate need of a pick-me-up. Homegirl had a lot of nerve running up on her the way she dld. Chyna was proud of herself. The old Chyna would've beat the shit out of her and then asked questions later.

Chyna was glad that she didn't go crazy on her. She had fucked the girl's husband. Chyna knew the feeling all too well of losing your mind behind a no-good-ass nigga. She'd been Selena way too many times to count. She hoped Selena would stop pretending to be 007 and find the strength to leave his sorry-ass alone before she got fucked up for real. Chyna didn't have time to focus her energy on Selena and her mess. She'd set her straight and thankfully would never have to see her again.

It was time to party. Chyna hated to be alone. Smoking blunt after blunt and going out high off Xanax had been fun but lonely. She wanted her daughter to come home. India gave her purpose. When India was home the weed and pills were put to the side. Chyna seemed to be more focused.

Her book was still on the back burner. She wasn't excited by the notion of sitting in front of a computer screen writing a sixty to ninety-thousand-word book. She wanted to tell stories in a different way. Chyna didn't know how she was going to get her foot through the door but she was determined to get her SAG card.

Since she wasn't in the mood to write, she decided to do reviews on the Starz hit series Power. Chyna had been a huge fan of season 1. Season 2 had just started and she had already begun filming her reviews. To her surprise, she'd gotten a great response from the viewers and over 8,000 views on the first two videos.

She was ecstatic. She'd never gotten that many views on one of her All Tea, All Shade videos. She couldn't wait to see if the views would continue to rise. Filming her Power reviews had been a welcome distraction from not being able to write and missing India and Carlos. It was hard for her to get sleep at night. Memories of him haunted her. She wondered if she had even ran across his mind in the two weeks they'd been apart.

He hadn't reached out to her. He knew where she stayed. If he wanted to see her, he would've swung by, but he didn't. Chyna hated that she even cared. She so wanted him to be a non-muthafuckin' factor in her life but he had her dickmatized. She wanted him in the worst way.

She missed their conversations. Carlos made it so easy for her to open up to him. She hadn't met a man that she felt was on her level mentally, financially, sexually and spiritually. Most dudes were idiots, liars, phonies and broke. Chyna was used to running the show. Carlos matched her fly in every way. He knew how to take control of her. He knew how to put her in her place. Tyreik couldn't even do that.

Chyna stood posted up against the wall with her people. She was on her fly shit. She was by far one of the baddest chicks in the room. She rocked a pair of cat-eye, Quay sunnies with a black matte lip. Yes, she wore her sunglasses inside. Chyna was extra like that. A black, jersey, Alexander Wang, spaghetti-strapped dress kissed every curve of her body. The sides dipped down to her waist exposing the sides of her boobs. The back of the dress was completely out. Highlighting her black pedicured toes were a pair of black, suede, caged-designed, lace-up, single-sole heels. Midi rings decorated each of her fingers.

Chyna's 28-inch stiletto nails were painted matte black as well. You couldn't tell her she wasn't the shit. She was surrounded by art and felt like she was a piece herself. Chyna was in her element. She was on her second Jack and Coke. Whenever she was beat to capacity, buzzed and grooving to good music, she felt invincible. The only thing that would make the night extra lit is if she got some dick.

She hadn't been dicked down since the last time she and Carlos had sex. For some reason she felt like if she smashed somebody else she'd be cheating on him. Unknowingly, her pussy had become his personal property. She honestly didn't want to give it to anyone else. Only he could make her cum multiple times and still have her craving more. *I gotta get this cracker out my mind*, Chyna took a sip from her red cup.

"Everybody in this muthafucka tonight." Brooke said thoroughly enjoying herself.

"Yeah, too many people for me," Asia added on edge.

She hated being in crowded places with Jaylen. He was constantly bombarded with people asking for pictures and autographs. Asia studied the crowd. It was way too many dudes in the spot with a hint of jealousy in their eyes. Niggas in St. Louis were hungry and looking for any way to eat. Asia may not have lived there anymore but she was fully aware of the senseless violence that went on.

She didn't need anybody trying Jaylen just so they could have a come up. He was iced out and draped in designer duds. Her husband was the 100 million dollar man and everyone in the room knew it. Asia didn't want to take any chances. She wanted to get out of there. Jaylen took heed of her worries.

"We'll get up outta here in a minute." He kissed her on the forehead.

Asia's happiness was his main concern.

"It's lit in here. You trippin'." Chyna turned up as Total's *Can't You See* came on.

"Awwwww shit! This our song!" Brooke danced with her.

Asia quickly joined in. When they were teenagers they used to pretend that they were the group members. Asia was Kima, Chyna was Keisha and Brooke was Pam.

"In the middle of the day now, baby... I seem to think of only you... Never thinkin' for a moment, baby... That you've been thinkin' of me too." Chyna, Brooke and Asia Diddy bopped together like they were in the music video.

Every time Chyna heard the song she became lost in the sickening beat. She was in the zone. The bass was booming and she couldn't stop grooving. She felt the vibrations from the speakers all through her body. This was exactly what the doctor ordered. Chyna had every intention on getting drunk and poppin' her pussy for a real nigga.

She had to figure out who the lucky fella would be. There was a cute chocolate brother that had been eye-fuckin' her since she'd walked through the door. He looked like he was working with a monster but Chyna wasn't sure. There was something that read **stage 5 clinger alert** about him. She didn't have any time for that. She didn't need to be around anyone that was going to bring down her high.

Chyna scanned the venue for another potential fuck buddy. The place was dimly lit so it was kind of hard to make out the different faces in the room. It didn't help that she was wearing sunglasses either. There was one face however that she would be able to make out anywhere. She'd studied every crevice of it. Chyna took off her shades so she could get a better look at him.

She and Carlos locked eyes and time stood still. Everyone around them moved in slow motion. Chyna drank him in. She wanted to savor every part of him. The man's swag was on overload. He was tanner than before but a little extra melanin in his skin was good. Like the rapper G-Eazy, his hair was slicked back and tapered on the sides.

He donned a black denim jacket, black Opening Ceremony t-shirt, black Balmain ripped jeans and black low-top Vans. Chyna wanted nothing more than to rid herself of her clothes and leap into his arms. The music, wetness between her thighs and him was a dangerous combination. She couldn't front, he was the one she wanted to go home with. He was her drug of choice.

Carlos licked his bottom lip and eyed her seductively. He hadn't expected to run into her but was glad he had. He'd thought about her every second of the day since she left. He didn't mean to be an asshole and not say goodbye. He was in his feelings and his jealousy had reared its ugly head. He wanted to treat her like the other women he came in contact with but Chyna wasn't like the rest. She was unlike any woman he'd ever met before.

She knew how to get under his skin. She knew exactly what buttons to push. She didn't know it but she was his kryptonite. Sometimes he hated that he bumped into her that night at Mango. His life was less complicated before her. After coming in contact with her everything went to hell. He was just now getting his life back on track. He didn't need Chyna coming back and fucking things up all over again.

She was the devil draped in a black dress. The way she looked should've been a sin. The fabric of the dress clung to her breasts and hips like glue. Carlos didn't like how exposed she was. He could see how hard her nipples were all the way across the room. She needed to be spanked. Visions of him taking her from behind and slapping her round, juicy ass while she screamed his name filled his mind. Carlos tried to shake the nasty thoughts in his brain. He had to figure out if he was drawn to Chyna or her pussy. She had him willing to go against his rules and allow himself to catch feelings.

"Ain't that yo' boo?" Brooke pointed out.

"Yeah, that's him." Chyna stood up straight and placed her shoulders back.

"Ooooh, Chyna, he's even cuter now," Asia beamed. "You better stop playing and lock that man down."

"You gon' say hi?" Brooke nudged her arm.

"Yeah, I guess. How do I look?" She posed.

"Bitch, you know you cute." Brooke twisted her lips to the side.

"A'ight, I'll be right back." Chyna popped a piece of gum in her mouth.

She was fully prepared to swallow her pride and make the first move. Her ego was quickly cracked when she spotted Bellamy walk up behind Carlos and wrap her arms around his waist. Carlos looked over his shoulder at her as she smiled wickedly and kissed his cheek. Chyna's nostrils flared. *No he didn't bring this big head bitch here with him,* she fumed feeling stupid.

Bellamy rested her chin on Carlos' shoulder and glared at Chyna. She had to let her know that she had no chance in hell of being with Carlos. He was hers and always would be. They shared a bond that could never be broken or infiltrated. Bellamy could have Carlos whenever she wanted and vice versa. They had that kind of power over each other. Whatever he and Chyna shared could never compare. The sooner she learned that she was just another fling, the better off they all would be. Bellamy grinned devilishly at Chyna and winked her eye. Chyna had never been so embarrassed in her life.

"Girl, who is that bitch hugging all up on him?" Asia questioned, mad.

"His ex." Chyna clenched her jaw.

The fact that Bellamy felt comfortable enough to greet him like that spoke volumes. All that shit he talked about them being done and over was bullshit. Carlos was just like every other man she'd run into. She couldn't believe a word that came out of his fuckin' mouth.

She felt like a complete dummy for taking his word at face value and believing it. She knew better. That was rule 101 in the playa handbook. Never believe shit a man tell you. Chyna hadn't let a man run game on her in years.

She for damn sure wasn't about to start now. She was too old for this bullshit.

"Fall back, man." Carlos' voice dripped venom.

He knew Bellamy was trying to be funny on purpose.

"What? You don't want yo' li'l girlfriend to get mad?" She unlocked her arms and stood in his face.

"You didn't want me so why you care?" He spat.

Bellamy's heart dropped out of her chest as he left her standing there.

Carlos made his way across the room to Chyna. He could see she was upset. He secretly delighted in the fact that she was jealous.

"Ooooh, girl, he's coming over." Asia pulled Chyna's arm enthusiastically.

"Calm down," Chyna jerked her arm away. "I don't know what he's coming over here for." She fixed her dress once more. "He can keep his li'l white ass over there wit' Princess Jasmine." She sucked her teeth.

Her heart raced a mile a minute as he neared.

"What's up, pretty girl? You look beautiful." He greeted her with a soft kiss on the cheek.

Chyna's chest heaved up-and-down. She hated that she was so affected by his touch. She was even madder that she felt some type of way about seeing him with another woman. Maybe she was just mad 'cause the other woman was Bellamy.

"I know I look cute. What you want?" She snapped with an attitude.

"I just came over to say hi, see what was up wit' you." Carlos looked down at her face.

He'd never seen her so upset.

"Ok... you spoke... bye." Chyna dismissed him.

She wanted to embarrass him the way he'd embarrassed her. Finding her funny, Carlos grinned and said, "You be good, Chyna." If she wanted him gone he'd gladly chuck her up the deuce. He wasn't fazed by her antics one bit. Chyna watched as he headed towards the door. Bellamy followed close behind him as he left the building. Seeing them leave together further fueled the rage she had inside.

"Damn, girl, you ain't have to do him like that," Asia said astonished by her brash behavior.

"Fuck that. Did you not just see him leave with that bitch?" Chyna quipped.

"I'm wit' you, friend. Don't come tryin' to be all up in my face then leave with another bitch," Brooke agreed.

"Girl, I'm so mad right now I don't know what to do." Chyna's face burned red.

"Why? You don't wanna be in a relationship, remember?" Asia reminded her.

"Shut up, Asia. Ain't nobody ask for your two cents." Chyna rolled her eyes so hard they almost popped out.

"I'm just sayin'; you can't get mad. Y'all not together."

"Yes the fuck I can and I am!" Chyna shrieked. "Carlos can kiss my black ass. He ain't never gotta worry

about hearing from me again. I put that on my daughter,"
she swore.

"You got it all on my face. I love the way that it tastes." – Tank, "Fuckin' Wit' Me"

#14

Brooke turned her headlights off and creeped down the street slowly. A soft glow from the streetlights lit the long concrete road. Chyna knew after Art, Beats + Lyrics that she should've went home but her anger had taken over. She had to check a muthafucka. Carlos had her all the way fucked up if he thought she was gonna sit back and watch him leave the event with his ex. She couldn't let that shit slide. Sure, she might've been overstepping her boundaries by poppin' up at his crib unannounced and in the wee hours of the morning, but in Chyna's mind, she had every right to.

He'd looked her dead in the face almost two weeks prior and said that he and Bellamy were over. She'd been nothing but honest about where she was at in her life. If he was still feeling ole girl, then that was all he had to say. She would've understood. She knew how it felt to still be hung up on an ex. It wasn't like she was his girl or was trying to be. All she asked for was honesty. She hated when muthafuckas didn't keep it 100.

Chyna hated liars. Lying to her was a sure way to be X'd out of her life permanently. She didn't have the time nor the patience for it. Brooke looked over at her friend as they pulled up to Carlos' crib. Chyna had begged her to stop by on the way home. Brooke knew better. Chyna said she just wanted to do a drive-by to see if he was home but Brooke was no dummy. She'd seen that deranged look in her friend's eyes before. She'd been on one too many of these missions with her in the past when she was dealing with Tyreik. Chyna was up to something.

"That's his house right there." She tapped Brooke on the arm.

All of the lights were off inside. His car was also parked out front. What she died to know was if he was alone.

"Stop the car!" She shouted scaring the shit outta Brooke.

Brooke quickly slammed on the brakes as her head slightly jerked back.

"Bitch, are you crazy? You can't be yelling out of nowhere like that!" She scolded her.

"I'll be right back." Chyna jumped out before Brooke could knock some sense into her.

"If he call the police on yo' dumb-ass, I'm leaving!" Brooke yelled out the window.

"Shhhhhhhh!" Chyna hissed.

She didn't want Carlos to know she was there. She wanted to pull a sneak attack on that ass. Chyna's veins pumped lava as she tiptoed up the steps. Using her fist, she pounded on the door and rang the doorbell at the same time. If he was inside fucking Bellamy she was going to make sure he didn't get a chance to bust a nut. Carlos' eyes popped open as he heard the loud banging at his door.

"What the fuck?" He groaned, rolling over and checking the time.

It was almost one o'clock. Enraged, he slipped out of bed naked and headed to the door. He hoped whoever was at his door acting a fool had life insurance 'cause they were about to die.

"Who is it?" He barked swinging open the door.

Chyna swallowed hard. She wasn't prepared for him to come to the door fully naked with his dick hanging midair. Her worst fear had come true. Bellamy was there getting her back cracked. Carlos was giving her dick away. *Lying muthafucka,* she thought.

"What the fuck do you want?" He snapped.

"Uhhhh, you can get the bass up out yo' voice," Chyna came back to her senses.

"Why are you banging on my damn door like you the fuckin' police? Are you crazy?" Carlos questioned, angrily.

He hated being woken up out of his sleep, especially behind some bullshit.

"You're the second person to call me crazy tonight." Chyna started to wonder if it was true.

"'Cause you are!"

"Whatever, you know you ain't have to lie to me, right?" She cocked her head to the side.

"Lie to you about what?" He sighed exasperated.

"About Bellamy. If you still had feelings for her, then you could've said that. Here you had me thinking it was over between y'all and in reality y'all still fuckin' around." Chyna swung her head from side-to-side like she had a head full of long weave.

"What the fuck are you talkin' about?" Carlos said confused.

"Oh, now you wanna play dumb?" She squinted her eyes. "Just like a nigga."

"What?" Carlos screwed up his face.

"You gon' act like I ain't see that bitch all over you? Then y'all left together and you in there fuckin' her right now! Or is she in a dick coma from all the long dick you gave her?" Chyna stood back on one leg and pursed her lips. *So that's what she wants,* Carlos thought eying her hard nipples.

"You out yo' fuckin' mind?" He stepped out onto the porch so he could make sure she understood how angry he was.

Chyna stepped back in fear of what he might do. Any man that didn't give zero fucks about stepping outside naked to check a bitch was certifiably crazy. Brooke watched the show down from her car, thoroughly amused. Now she understood why Chyna was so obsessed. Carlos had a body out of this world. She could see his chiseled six-pack in the dark. The myth about white men having small dicks was most certainly not true. Homeboy was working with a monster.

"Don't ever come out yo' mouth and call me the N word, you understand?" He pointed his finger to her head like a gun. "And ain't nobody lie to you. I'm a grown-ass fuckin' man. If I was fuckin' wit' Bellamy, I would've said that. And I didn't leave with her. I'm in this muthafucka by myself."

"You're not?" Chyna replied feeling stupid. "Thank God," she grinned, holding her chest.

"No, I'm not; but you need to fall the fuck back and chill. Don't ever come over here with that shit," he warned.

"My bad." Chyna said feeling like an idiot.

"Nah, fuck that. You ain't sorry but you gon' learn today." He yanked her by the arm. "Tell yo' li'l friend bye," he ordered.

"Brooke, I'ma call you later!" Chyna shouted over her shoulder as he drug her into the house.

Carlos didn't give her enough time to gather her thoughts or prepare for what was about to happen next. He was on a mission. He didn't give a fuck about nothing. He had to prove a point. With expert precision, he slid down her body and pushed the hem of her dress up over her hips. Carlos placed a trail of sensuous kisses all over her thighs. Chyna inhaled deep as he stood up and pushed her head down.

She thought he wanted her to pleasure him with her mouth, which excited her, but instead he flipped her over so her legs landed on his shoulders. Her pussy was right in his face. This was it. He was finally going to give her head. Carlos took his first taste of the sugariness between her thighs and fell in love. Her clit was as smooth as red velvet cake.

Chyna held onto him as he ate her pussy while standing up. He was giving her the best head she'd ever had. She tried to steady her breathing but each flicker of his tongue made her hyperventilate. It was all too much. Carlos gripped her thighs like they were Vise-Grips. He would never have his full of her. She drove him mad but a lesson had to be learned - that he wasn't to be fucked with.

With no warning he flipped her over again. Chyna's face was now planted in front of his erect dick. Her thighs rested on his shoulders while her heels were up in the air. She'd never been in the 69 position while a man was standing up. Carlos held her body in the air with one arm.

"You done being a fuckin' brat?" He slapped her hard on the ass with his free hand.

"Yes." Chyna panted.

"No you not. Stop lying." Carlos walked into the kitchen and opened the cabinet.

He pulled out a bottle of honey. Chyna didn't know what he was up to but was enjoying every second of it. Carlos squeezed the honey on her clit and watched as it slid down the slit of her pussy like rainwater. Hungrily, he dove in face first. The warmth from the honey and the wetness of his tongue had Chyna crying out to God. If this was what being a brat got her, then she would act up more often.

Each thrust of his tongue caused her nipples to sprout. His tongue was as lethal as a grenade. The only thing that kept her in one piece was by placing his thick rod in her mouth. Chyna needed something to muffle her cries. Carlos struggled not to cum. Chyna's whimpers and moans were driving him mad. Her warm mouth was swallowing his dick whole. Her oral game was a kaleidoscope of magical wonder.

He felt like he was tripping out. His hard cock was about to explode. Chyna sucked his entire dick as the tip hit the back of her throat. Carlos continued to annihilate her pussy with his tongue as his nut built. He could kiss her forever. He'd eat it from top to bottom if she wanted him to. Her juices dripped from his chin.

She was a sweet, sticky mess. He could no longer pretend he didn't want her. Lord knows he tried to resist. He'd tried to forget her but he couldn't hide from her hypnotic gaze. There was no dodging it. He could never resist her. She was his and he was hers.

Carlos and Chyna made love in the kitchen for hours. By the time they stopped the sun was up and birds were chirping. She sat in front of him as he fed her strawberries lathered in whipped cream. They both were sticky from the honey. Chyna had honey all over her. It was in places she didn't know she'd be able to clean.

"If you keep fuckin' me like this I'ma fuck around and get pregnant and Lord knows I don't want no more kids," she joked, telling a bold-faced lie.

A part of Chyna longed to have a second child.

"You ain't gotta worry. I haven't nutted up in you and don't plan on," Carlos stated bluntly, placing a strawberry up to her luscious lips.

His dick jumped with delight as she licked the tip. He loved that Chyna was just as nasty as him.

"You don't want kids?" She took a bite of the strawberry.

"Nah," Carlos said solemnly.

Thoughts of his son crossed his mind.

"Why not? You don't want a Carlos, Jr. or a baby girl that looks just like you running around?" She said shocked by his revelation.

"Kids ain't in my future and neither is marriage," he confessed.

"Why? When we met you said you wanted kids. What changed?"

This was the time for him to tell Chyna the truth. She deserved to know that when he first met her he was married to Bellamy. They'd been separated at the time for nearly a year. After nearly fifteen years of being together, their relationship ran its course. They grew apart. Her life was going one way and his another. Bellamy's ad agency was thriving and his business ventures were doing extremely well. With their busy schedules they were rarely around each other, and when they were, they spent all of their time arguing.

Fertility issues plagued their marriage as well. They'd tried everything from IVF to a surrogate to no avail. So after much deliberation and heartache, they decided to divorce. Carlos had plans on telling Chyna when they first met but she pulled a disappearing act and he never got the chance. Heartbroken that she'd cut him out of her life so abruptly, he sought affection from the only other woman he ever desired.

Despite all of their issues, Bellamy was his safe haven. Everything about them was familiar and safe. Bellamy got pregnant soon after they started back messing around. They both took it as a sign that they should try their hand at love once more. Carlos looked at her pregnancy like a sign from God that with her was where he needed to be. Any thoughts or feelings he had for Chyna were quickly placed on the back burner.

He and Bellamy moved back in together and called off the divorce. Carlos was on cloud nine. Nothing could shake his joy. He had everything a man could want. Then one day his world came crashing down around him. Bellamy was seven months pregnant. She woke up one morning with blood covering the sheets and her thighs. Carlos rushed her to the hospital. The doctors performed and emergency C-section on her in hopes of saving her and the baby.

She'd lost so much blood they thought she was going to die. Thankfully the doctors were able to stabilize her but the baby was still in trouble. He was born premature and his lungs weren't fully developed. He had to fight for every piece of air he breathed. Carlos never left his son's side as he lay helpless inside an incubator with tubes coming from every direction.

He was so tiny and fragile but Carlos loved him all the same. He'd waited his entire life to be a dad. His only desire was to hold him. He and Bellamy had so much faith that he'd make a full recovery that they named him and prepared for him to come home. Unfortunately, after only two weeks of living, baby Dash Christianson died.

When Dash died Carlos lost his will to go on as well. No baby deserved to die. Carlos would've gladly taken his place but life didn't work that way. He got to go on living knowing his son never had a fighting chance. Carlos took the loss of his son hard but Bellamy was distraught. She couldn't even think straight. She carried him for seven months and felt his little kicks.

After the burial, she sank into a deep depression. She suffered from postpartum. Carlos had somehow morphed from her lover into her opponent overnight. He secretly had begun to despise her too. They both blamed each other for the death of their son when it was neither of their fault. Needless to say, things between them went from bad to worse.

Carlos couldn't keep up with her erratic behavior. Bellamy couldn't stop crying and tearing up the house. She hated herself for not being able to carry her baby full-term. She and Carlos couldn't stand each other. They were both mirror images of what their son could've been. After a few months of destroying each other, Bellamy put Carlos out and begged for a divorce.

Carlos hated her for throwing him away. He was still all in but he was tired of fighting. Instead of fighting each other, he wanted to fight for their marriage. But since Bellamy was so unhappy, he threw in the towel and gave her what she wanted. Before Carlos could blink, they were divorced and he was left mourning the death of his son and his marriage.

It had only been six months since the ink on his and Bellamy's divorce papers dried. So much had transpire that he didn't know if Chyna would fully understand where he was at mentally. Hell, sometimes Carlos didn't understand himself. The only thing he knew for sure was that after the death of his son he refused to love anything or anyone. He'd been hurt enough.

Chyna had already been dogged by her ex. He didn't want to be another man to enter her life and wreak havoc. He didn't want her to think that he was playing games or trying to play with her heart. But if he told her the truth now, that's exactly what she would think. It would look like he came into the picture with nothing but ill intentions which was the farthest thing from the truth.

"That's a story for another day." He leaned over and kissed her cheek.

"Now it seems like your interest ain't here." – Destiny's Child, "Is She The Reason"

#15

For five days straight Chyna and Carlos did nothing but fuck, eat great food and party. She got to go to his tattoo shops, see the layout and meet the artists. Seeing his team of tattoo artists and their level of work and professionalism was a sheer indication of how good of a businessman he was. Knowing his background and how hard he had to work to get to where he was made Chyna fall for him even more.

Carlos was the true definition of the American dream. She could tell by the grateful look in his eye that he was thankful for all of his blessings. Chyna related to his gratitude. She too came from nothing and made something. She cherished all of the things God had given her. That's why after five days of being with him, she had to breakaway and focus on her own career.

She had to film her Power review video, edit it and load it onto YouTube which was a ten-hour process. After watching that week's episode at midnight on Starz On

Demand, she filmed until 3:00am, then got up early that Saturday morning to edit the video. She liked to have the video up by mid-afternoon so that her subscribers who watched at midnight like her could watch early.

It was a lot of hard work but Chyna enjoyed the process of sharing her thoughts and views with her audience. She was so happy that she'd struck a chord with an audience who loved to watch the show as much as she did. With the large viewership came a ton of new subscribers. The Color Me Pynk channel was finally blowing up and gaining recognition.

Chyna was thrilled her YouTube career was doing great because her career as an author was still on the fritz. She still hadn't come up with a plot line for her next book. Time was ticking and she had to start writing soon. Chyna sat at her computer and opened her Windows Movie Maker. She was all ready to start editing when she heard the doorbell ring.

Chyna wasn't expecting any visitors. She had no idea who was at the door. Chyna stood up and took a quick glance at what she wore. She was still dressed in her pajamas. She wore a slouchy t-shirt, no bra and white boy shorts. Normally, she'd throw on a bra but that morning she didn't feel like it. Whoever was at her door was going to be sent away so it didn't matter. Chyna jogged down the steps and cautiously looked out the blinds.

"Oh hell no." She fumed pissed.

It was Selena. Chyna unlocked the door and opened it.

"What the hell do you want?" She looked around to see if she was alone.

She was.

"Why are you at my house? Do you wanna die?" She got up in Selena's face.

As soon as she did she realized that Selena wasn't the same, put together girl she'd seen two weeks before. She looked a mess. She looked pale and sick. Her beautiful, long, bouncy hair was now greasy and stringy. Mascara was running down her face from crying so much. Homegirl needed Jesus, Blue Ivy and a hug ASAP.

"No-no-no don't be mad. I come in peece. See, I bought coffee and donuts." Selena held up a brown bag and tray of drinks.

Chyna eyed her suspiciously. Anybody that knew her knew the way to her heart was food. She loved to eat. *Those donuts sure do smell good*, she thought. *Don't you eat that shit. Her crazy-ass might be tryin' to poison you.*

"How do you even know where I stay, Britney Spears?"

"I followed ju home after ju left the rest-ter-aunt," Selena replied sheepishly.

"Ok... see, I'ma have to get a restraining order against yo' crazy-ass and, girl, you are way too pretty to be so damn crazy," Chyna exclaimed.

"I swear to ju I'm not crazy. I jes veally need jur help." Selena bounced from one foot to another.

"Help with what, Lindsey Lohan?"

"Can I peassse come in?"

Chyna looked her up-and-down. The donuts were calling her name.

"Let me tell you something." She got up into Selena's personal space. "Try me if you want to. I beat bitches up for fun and please believe I got the four-four waiting by the doe."

"I don't no what this foe-foe is but I promise ju won't have any prob-lems out of me. Jur my friend," Selena smiled, sincerely.

"See, that's where you got the game fucked up. I am not your friend." Chyna snatched the bag of donuts from her hand and walked back into the house.

Selena was hot on her tail.

"Uh huh, ju are my only friend in Saint Louis." She dragged out the word. "But why ju got so many steps?" Selena tried to catch her breath as she entered Chyna's kitchen.

"Don't talk about my steps, Rosie Perez!" Chyna took a bite out of a glazed donut. "Now what you want?"

"Who?" Selena asked her confused.

"What you want, girl?" Chyna groaned annoyed. "And you better be happy I ain't got no man up in here 'cause you really would've got cussed out."

"I need jur help with Waymon. I no he's cheating on me. I jes need poof."

"Proof," Chyna corrected her.

"Poof," Selena repeated, slowly.

"Proof!"

"Poof." Selena tried to enunciate.

"Whatever," Chyna flicked her wrist. "What you mean you need proof? I'm right here."

"I need to find out who Waymon's mattresses is?"

"Mistress?" Chyna questioned confused.

"Jes, that word," Selena snapped her finger.

"I understand that there's a language barrier here but you do realize I fucked yo' husband, right? You have to know how weird this is?"

"Whoever dis woman is he's spending a lot of money on her," Selena continued. "I found receipts from Victoria Secret and Tiff-any's. He even took her to Red Lobster. He knows that's my favorite place. And I don't no anyone here besides my cou-zin Loupita. And she's getting married in a few weeks so she won't help me. All I have is ju. I have no friends to talk to," Selena started to cry.

"All of my family is in Mi-ami. My dog Pedro is sick. I broke one of my nails." She held up her hand. "And my nail tech is out-of-town so I can't get it fixed. And Waymon leaves me in the house all the time. I'm always alone. Jur the only person I no. And jur so strong and confident and mean. Jur like the baddest bitch I know. Jur like Trina. Jur the baddest bitch."

"Well, you are right about that." Chyna tossed her imaginary long hair over her shoulder. "I am the baddest bitch," she beamed. "But that's not the point. First of all, you need to stop crying. It's not a good look for you. Second, I ain't tryin' to get caught up in yo' mess. I got my own shit to deal with."

"Please," Selena fell out on the floor. "I don't no what else to do. I can't stay married to a man that is cheating on me. I thought Waymon married me because he loved me. I've knew hem since I was born. We grew up together. We were best friends. We were arranged by our parents to be married. In the beginning everything was great. We used to do everything together. We used to go shopping all the time. He used to help me pick out my outfits. I was his little princess. Now he acts like he doesn't even no me anymore. I don't no what I did wrong. He barely touches me."

"Yeah, that nigga cheating," Chyna verified.

Only a man that was fucking another woman would pass up the opportunity to bang Selena. There was defiantly a stranger in her house.

"But what is up with you and falling out on the floor all the time? Is that like a Puerto Rican thing? Let me know," Chyna turned up her face.

"No it's not," Selena hiccuped as she cried.

"Well then you need to cut it. Be a woman and cry on the inside like the rest of us."

Selena tried to keep her tears inside but found it too difficult. She felt like she was drowning from the inside.

"I can't; it makes my head hurt," she wept.

"Oh my God," Chyna scratched her head.

"I jes need ju to be my ride or die."

"I don't even know you, Selena Gomez."

"What do ju need to know?" Selena sat up. "My name is Selena Lopez. I'm twenty-eight years old. I was born and raised in Mi-ami. I don't have any children and I'm a licensed massage therapist."

"You do massages?" Chyna arched her brow.

"Jes."

"Shit, you should've said that at first. Ok, I'll help you but I'ma needed snacks and you're gonna owe me a deep tissue massage." Chyna held out her hand.

"Bet!" Selena spit on her hand then tried to give Chyna a shake.

"Bitch, you done lost yo' mind." Chyna smacked her hand away.

"Right in front of me but my vision is blurred." – Jazmine Sullivan, "Veins"

#16

All of the lights were off. White, vanilla-scented candles were lit. Flickers of light from the flames danced across the ceiling but Chyna couldn't see any of it. A black satin scarf covered her eyes. The heat from the candles warmed her skin. Carlos was really pushing her boundaries. She somehow had agreed to allow him to tie her wrists to his headboard while she lie fully exposed.

Chyna had never done anything so daring and risqué before. She'd fucked in public, on balconies and in cars but never had she given someone complete control over her body. Carlos was driving her insane and he hadn't even touched her yet. Chyna was officially addicted to him. This crazy, intoxicating thing they shared was surely going to be the death of her. She was in complete anticipation of what was in store. All of her senses were high on alert. Each time she heard his footsteps across the floor she got thrilled.

Carlos sipped on his chilled glass of Pinot Noir and watched as Chyna fidgeted. She had no idea how much he was enjoying watching her voluptuous frame gleam under the candlelight. Her honey-colored skin looked so soft and smooth. She was perfect in every way imaginable which was the problem. He was falling for her and falling for her was not in the plan.

He didn't want her to be his girlfriend but they were more than friends. He made love to her but refused to call her his lover. He never took for granted any time they spent together but he was unwilling to give them a title. His actions spoke louder than any words he could ever speak with his lips. If Carlos gave a voice to the feelings he had inside, then that would make them real.

He'd never promised her anything but good dick and a good time so he could never be held accountable for anything outside of that. They'd both sworn that neither of them wanted to be in a relationship. What they were doing was working for the both of them. What was in a name anyway?

He wasn't fucking with anyone else. Fucking her was the shit to him. She was the only one he thought of. He made sure that Chyna was nothing but happy when she was in his presence. He treated her with the utmost respect and showered her with affection but that was as far as things would go. At least that's what he tried to tell himself.

Carlos turned on his Beats Pill+ to set the mood. Tank's sultry, commanding voice set the tone for the night. Carlos took one more sip of wine then picked up a bottle of massage oil. Chyna had no idea what she was in store for. He had some fun things in store for her that night. Carlos eased onto the bed and proceeded to squirt the strawberry-scented oil over her body.

Carlos watched her bite her bottom lip as he massaged her nipples. Chyna quivered under his touch. She was so turned on she couldn't stand it. Her hard nipples glided through his long fingers with ease. Her breasts reminded him of two perfect mounds of flesh that he wanted to bury his face in. Carlos picked up the oil and parted Chyna's legs. He squirted a generous amount onto the face of her pussy.

Carlos delicately began to massage her pussy lips with his fingertips. Chyna couldn't help but release a soft moan. His fingers were working magic on her clit. Carlos' dick got harder with each of her moans. She wasn't loud enough though. He needed her to get louder. He wanted the neighbors to hear her cries so he inserted two of his fingers inside her wet slit. Chyna's stomach contracted as he drove his oiled fingers deep inside her canal. She wanted so badly to see his face as he played with her pussy.

"You like that?" He asked fucking her pussy with his fingers while thumbing her clit.

"Yessssssss, it feels so good," she cried out rotating her hips.

Chyna had never been so wet in her life.

"Carlos!" She yelled as he hit her spot.

"Yes, baby." He replaced his thumb with his tongue, sending her into a tailspin.

"I wanna see you," Chyna squirmed, feeling herself about to cum.

Carlos couldn't even respond. He was too transfixed on how her body was responding to his touch. Her nipples were calling his name. Goosebumps covered her skin. She was about to burst and Carlos was going to enjoy every second of it by lapping up her sweet juices as she came.

"Oooooh, Carlos," Chyna pinched her eyes shut. "Oooh, baby! I can't take it! It feels so good!" She grinded her hips to the rhythm of his finger strokes.

Just as she was about to cum, Carlos released his fingers and lathered her entire pussy with his tongue. His tongue traveled from her clit to her lips to inside her warm hole. Chyna screamed out in agony. Carlos savored every drop as her body quacked. Once she settled from her orgasmic high, he pushed the scarf up over her eyes so she could see. Chyna blinked her eyes until her vision was focused. Not being able to use her hands was killing her.

"Baby, untie me," she begged.

"Not yet." Carlos got off the bed and grabbed a box from his closet.

Chyna eyed him with a sinful look of lust in her eyes. She wanted him inside of her in the worst way.

"I got something for you." He said opening the box.

Chyna lay helpless as he pulled out a stack of Cartier LOVE bracelets. He'd gotten her two pink gold bracelets with diamonds and a pink gold bracelet with pink sapphires. Chyna's mouth dropped open. The two pink gold bracelets cost $14,600 a piece and the pink gold bracelet with pink sapphires cost $16,000. Cartier LOVE bracelets were a big thing. Once you put them on they couldn't come off unless you had the screw that came along with it. They were a gorgeous token of love.

No one had ever bought Chyna something so extravagant. She couldn't help but wonder if this was his way of saying he loved her. *Nah, he can't*, she thought. It's too soon. *No it's not. You know damn well you love him too*. Carlos took each of the bracelets out the box and opened them. He hoped that Chyna wouldn't look too much into the meaning behind him giving her such a thoughtful gift.

He'd seen them and thought of her. And yes, there was a special place in his heart reserved for her where love had begun to grow. She'd never know that. The lines between them were blurry enough.

"Carlos, are you kidding me? You got me the Cartier LOVE bracelets?" She beamed ecstatically. "They're beautiful."

"You're prettier." He said locking them onto her wrist.

Chyna smiled so hard her cheeks hurt. As he placed the last one onto her wrist, she quickly noticed a key hanging from the bracelet.

"Is that the key to take them off? I thought you had to use a screw?" She asked perplexed.

"No, it's a key to my place." He winked his eye.

"You want me to have a key to your place?" Chyna's eyes grew wide like saucers. "That's a big thing. You haven't even been to my crib since we started back fuckin' around."

"I know it's a big step but I like having you around." He eased between her legs.

"You sure?" Her heart pounded.

"Yeah, I'm sure." He kissed her lips.

"Well, I want you to have a key to my place too," she savored his taste.

Carlos admired her frame. Her body shined like a wet oil painting. She was his canvas. Carlos grabbed the massage oil and squirted some all over his dick. Chyna swallowed the huge lump in her throat. His long but thick dick stood at full attention. The massage oil dripped from the tip like rain. She wanted all ten inches of his hard cock inside her mouth.

"Baby, please let me touch it," she salivated. "I wanna taste it."

Carlos didn't even bother responding. He had her exactly where he wanted her. He simply slipped his dick inside her pussy and proceeded to work her middle.

"Awww fuck!" Chyna screamed as he held her waist and pounded her pussy.

Her titties bounced back and forth with each hard stroke. Carlos looked down at the golden brown girl that lie before him. The hold that Chyna had on him was stronger than rum fresh out of the bottle. If he didn't get a hold of his feelings things were sure to get out of hand. But every time she flashed her dimples, laughed, pouted or moaned, he became further entangled in her web.

He couldn't shake her and honestly didn't want to. The more his feelings grew, the harder it became to tell her the truth. *You cannot fall in love with her*, he told himself as he kissed her passionately. Chyna kissed him back with just as much intensity. Her head was up in the clouds. She was falling head over heels in love with him. Carlos had her wide open; literally. Her body was his to explore. He could do with her as he pleased and he did.

"Never seen a girl with an ass so fat." – Electrik Red, "Muah"

#17

It was the night of the stakeout. Chyna and Brooke were dressed and ready to go. It was 87 degrees outside but Chyna wore a black hoodie, black biker shorts and black and white Superstar Adidas. She needed to be incognito. Chyna didn't know what she was getting herself into but she was down for whatever. In case anything crazy popped off, she had Brooke there for backup.

"Girl, I can't believe you got me out here at eleven o'clock at night on a damn suicide mission," Brooke quipped as they headed towards Selena's car.

"You know you love to play Cagney and Lacey," Chyna joked.

"The bitch got a nice car." Brooke admired Selena's silver 2015 Audi R8.

"Hopefully she'll get it in the divorce," Chyna laughed.

"You ain't shit." Brooke cracked up laughing as Selena unlocked the doors. "Fake ass."

"Hey, girl. Where are my snacks?" Chyna asked getting inside.

"Hi," Selena spoke, looking back at Brooke as she got in the car. "Ju didn't tell me ju were bringing a friend."

"The more eyes the better, right?" Chyna pointed out. "Now, where are my snacks?" She asked impatiently.

"Hi, I'm Brooke," Brooke extended her hand.

"Ju are very pret-ty." Selena gave her a firm handshake.

"Thank you," Brooke blushed. "And I love your hair. It's so thick and pretty. Is it all yours or is that some virgin Remy?"

"Who is Remy?" Selena screwed up her face confused.

"Girl, ain't nobody got time to explain nothin' to Dora the Explorer," Chyna said in a huff. "We gotta get this show on the road. Now where is my food? A bitch is hungry." Her stomach growled.

"Here, I got ju some sushi." Selena handed her the plastic container. "And some chips and a bag of sour gummy worms per jur request."

"I swear you are my spirit animal." Chyna smiled with glee.

"Ok, so we're going to shoot by my house first 'cause Waymon will be leaving out soon."

"How you know he ain't already left yet?" Chyna wondered out loud.

"He always leaves out at the same time."

"Dumb-ass. He don't even try to switch his shit up. He must really think he got a fool on his hands," Brooke said in disbelief.

"Well, I'm going to show him tonight that I'm no dummy." Selena placed the car in drive and pulled off.

Minutes later they were parked down the block from her house. Like clockwork, Waymon left the house at

11:30. From the dip in his walk, Chyna could tell he thought he was the shit. Homeboy was draped from head to toe in True Religion. He wore a skin-tight, white tee with a gold horseshoe on the chest, a pair of True Religion, patchwork, jeans and the ugliest pair of doo-doo brown True Religion high-top tennis shoes she'd ever seen. Chyna wanted to vomit. She despised the gaudy, hood clothing line.

"Oh my God. I can't believe I ever slept with him," she scowled.

"I can't believe you did either." Brooke pretended to throw up.

"Hey!" Selena shouted with a look of horror on her face. "That's my husss-band ju talkin' about."

"You let him pick out your clothes, for real?" Chyna frowned. "'Cause that outfit he got on his terrible."

"I bought him that outfit!"

"It's ok. We all have our off days," Chyna assured, swallowing a piece of spicy salmon sushi.

"Yeah, girl. You don't know no better." Brooke patted Selena on the shoulder.

"Listen, Selena," Chyna turned and looked at her. "Anybody that wears head to toe True Religion stay slangin' dick."

"Ain't that the truth," Brooke agreed.

"You can't tell me this nigga ain't got kids all over St. Louis," Chyna added.

"Ju think so?" Selena replied, sadly.

"Yeah, baby girl." Chyna poked out her bottom lip. "That's what we're here for, to put you up on game."

"Ooh... he's on the move!" Brooke jumped up-and-down. "Step on it!"

Selena put her foot on the gas and tailed him.

"Where does he think you are?" Chyna asked.

"He thinks I'm at my cou-zins house helping her with her wedding decorations. I told him I'd be there all night."

"So does he go out every weekend?" Brooke probed.

"Jes and during the week too. He always leaves me behind. I ask him can I go out with him but he always says no."

"Girl, you don't need to follow him. I can tell you right now he's cheating," Chyna waved her off.

"I know he's cheating on me. I wanna catch him in the act. Dis girl he's seeing is really special to him 'cause he's always with her. She's taking all of my time. I jes don't no why he moved me here to do dis to me," Selena shrugged.

"'Cause that's what men do. They isolate you so you can't have nobody in yo' ear telling you the real. Waymon wanna do his cheating in peace, chile," Chyna laughed.

"Right," Brooke nodded her head as they parked down the street from club Envy.

Waymon valeted his car and walked inside.

"Now we wait." Selena made herself comfortable.

An hour and a half passed by and Waymon still hadn't emerged from the club. Chyna was starting to grow restless.

"Ok, Selena, girl. How long we gon' stay here and wait for him to come out? My legs are starting to hurt and I have run out of snacks." She held up the empty containers.

"My legs are starting to hurt too," Brooke yawned.

"Let's go home. You already know what it is, girl," Chyna tried to talk some sense into Selena.

"Ooooh ooh... there he is! He's coming out!" Selena started up the engine.

"I hope he goes straight home so you can drop my ass off." Chyna shot, placing on her seatbelt.

"He's not." Selena furrowed her brows as he hopped on the highway heading north. "He's going the opposite way."

"Aww shit! Now it's gettin' good!" Brooke rubbed her hands together excited.

Suddenly Selena's phone started to ring. The sound scared all of them.

"Oh shit! It's hem calling me!" She panicked.

"Answer the phone dammit!" Chyna threw it onto her lap like it was a hot potato.

"I don't no what to say!"

"Act natural! Act clueless like you always do," Chyna coached.

"Ok." Selena placed the call on speaker. "Hola, papi."

"Hey, baby. What you doing?"

"Ummm," Selena paused looking around frantically.

Chyna mimed her making centerpieces but Selena couldn't make out what she was doing.

"I'm ma-king em... panadas," she said unsure.

Chyna screwed up her face and looked at her like she was dumb. After rolling her eyes, she mimed herself doing decorations again.

"I mean, I'm making cen-terpieces," Selena smiled, getting it.

Chyna slumped down in her seat and wiped the invisible sweat from her brows. Selena was going to give her a heart attack.

"Y'all still up doing that shit? I thought y'all would be done by now."

"It's very stressful. I miss ju though, papi. What are ju doing?" Selena changed the subject.

"I'm on my way home. I'm tired than a muthafucka," Waymon lied, faking a yawn.

"This lying muthafucka!" Brooke shook her head. "He a dirty dog."

"Who was that?" Waymon asked, hearing someone in the background.

"Lupita. She was admiring one of the centerpieces I made." Selena pursed her lips at Brooke.

"A'ight, well I'm about to go in the house and go to bed. I'll see you in the morning when you come home."

"Ok, papi,. I love ju," Selena responded sweetly.

"Love you, too," Waymon ended the call.

"We gon' jump his ass." Chyna said amped as hell. "He's heading over that bitch house right now."

"Finally, I get to see who he's loving more than me," Selena replied, feeling sick to her stomach.

She thought she was ready to see what her husband was up to but now she wasn't so sure. She genuinely loved Waymon. He was her best friend. When she said "I Do", she thought they'd be married forever. Now everything around her was tumbling down. Inhaling deep, she followed his car into a residential neighborhood.

Selena didn't recognize the area. After a left and a right turn, he parked in front of a brick home. Selena turned off the headlights and watched as he walked inside the house. The door was already unlocked for him to come in.

"What you gon' do, Cindy Lou?" Chyna cocked her head to the side.

"Should I go knock on the door?" Selena asked nervously.

Her palms had begun to sweat.

"Hell naw! See, you got life fucked up. You just can't be walking up to people's house and knocking on the door. Just 'cause I didn't kick yo' ass don't mean the next bitch won't. This ain't Miami, girl. You in St. Louis. These niggas around here kill people for fun," Chyna explained.

"Just wait for him to come out then confront him," Brooke suggested, getting comfortable in the backseat.

An hour later they were still in the car waiting. Brooke had fallen asleep. Selena was in the driver's seat crying on the inside like Chyna had taught her and Chyna was texting Carlos. He was waiting on her to come by.

"Look, Selena, I know you're hurting but I got some dick waiting on me that I need to get to."

"Jes a li'l while longer peas," Selena pleaded.

"You already know he's cheating. I'm proof of that. Seeing this other bitch ain't gon' prove nothing that you don't already know."

"I jes need to see hem with her. I need to see it for my own eyes."

"You Spanish chicks are crazy." Chyna folded her arms across her chest. "You got twenty more minutes and then we're out of here."

"We don't even have to wait that long. He's coming out." Selena moved closer to the steering wheel so she could see better.

Chyna's eyes darted over to Waymon walking out of the girl's house, zipping up his jeans. A bald head chick dressed in a pink, silk robe followed behind him. The girl had a big ole Khloe Kardashian ass dragging behind her. Selena had never seen an ass so fat. Once he got to his car, Waymon leaned against the driver side door. The girl wrapped her arms around his neck and gave him a sloppy, wet kiss goodbye.

"Lousy, ningún buen hijo de puta," Selena spat in Spanish. "I'm going to kill hem!" She hopped out of the car.

"Selena! Wait!" Chyna called after her unprepared. "Brooke, wake up! It's about to go down!" Chyna jumped out as well.

Selena race-walked across the street. Her heels clicked against the pavement. Waymon and the girl were tonguing each other down so hard they didn't even hear her footsteps.

"Really, Waymon? I thought ju were going home?" Selena reached around the girl and hit him in the head.

Waymon's eyes popped open and the woman he was kissing spun around. Selena nearly passed out when she and what she assumed was a girl made eye contact. A tall, dark man with a platinum blonde buzz cut and grey contacts looked back at her.

"Jur a man?" She shrieked stunned.

"Polly wanna cracker? Waymon, who the hell is this salty fish?" Delicious popped his lips.

"I'm his wife!" Selena shouted, holding up her left hand.

"Wife?" Delicious jerked his head back. "What the hell you mean wife? Waymon, you married? And to a woman?" He clutched a set of invisible pearls.

"Hold up, baby. I can explain." Waymon stuttered in shock.

"Explain what? How you just got done fuckin' me in my ass?" Delicious pushed him in the chest.

"Oh my God. I think I'm gonna be sick." Selena held her stomach and hunched over.

"Selena! You alright?" Chyna ran up behind her and looked at Waymon and Delicious. "This nigga like dick?!" she screeched.

"Loooooves it," Delicious mouthed dramatically. "And who the hell are you?"

"Chile, I'm just an innocent bystander," Chyna responded.

She didn't want any part of this shit show.

"I can't believe you, Waymon. I gave you my heart and my asshole and this is how you do me? I stopped fuckin' Mario, Antonio, Kevin and Jamil for you! Mina said yo' ass wasn't shit!" Delicious pointed his finger in his face.

"Now you gon' have Mo and everybody at the shop laughing at me. You said we was gon' get married! I already started looking for my damn dress!" Delicious turned to Chyna. "Girl, I found this bad-ass, blush-colored, Vera Wang gown with a beaded bodice and fishtail bottom. And catch this tea, it was on sale for $4,000."

"Girl, really? Where at?" Chyna said intrigued.

She loved a good sale.

"At Kleinfeld's; can you believe that?" Delicious placed his hand on his hip.

"Umm, excuse ju two! I jes caught my husss-band cheating on me and with a man no less," Selena shouted angrily. "Ju two can talk fashion later!"

"Girl, you married to a man named Waymon! You ain't know he was gay?" Delicious shot.

"Selena, did you come here with her?" Waymon died to know.

"She sure did," Chyna replied, instead. "She knows all about me and you."

"Hold up... hold up... hold up!" Delicious bobbed his head from left-to-right. "You fuckin' her too? We just became homegirls!"

"Fucked... he fucked me one time." Chyna corrected him. "I ain't crazy enough to dip my toe back into that hot mess. This nigga look like all he loves is Hennessy and trap music."

"And what's wrong with that?" Waymon challenged.

"Well, when you put it like that, nothing," Chyna blinked.

"So you on the down low?" Delicious continued his line of questioning. "I'm yo' secret lover?" He teared up.

"Delicious, baby, you know I love you." Waymon took him into his arms and tried to make him understand.

"Nah, nigga, I'm through fuckin' wit' you," Delicious pushed him away. "I'm nobodies side bitch."

"Ju love hem?" Selena blacked out.

"What about me? I'm jur wife!" She punched him in the chest. "We've know each other our whole life!"

"I'VE BEEN GAY MY WHOLE LIFE! I THOUGHT YOU KNEW THAT! I like men and I like women!" Waymon screamed.

"Hell no I didn't no! Why would ju think I knew that? Well, that does explain why ju always liked to go shopping with me," Selena stopped to think.

Suddenly everything became crystal clear.

"I love you, Selena. You're like a sister to me but I'm in love with Delicious," Waymon explained.

"The devil is a lie! I don't want that kind of love and, sista-girl," Delicious turned to Selena. "You shouldn't either. You are far too pretty to be putting up with his bullshit. There are plenty more dicks in the sea."

"That's what I tried to tell her," Chyna spoke up.

"There are other ways to get a green card," Delicious verified.

"I'm a U.S. citizen," Selena cried.

"Oops, my bad!" Delicious placed his hand over his mouth.

"Damn, is it over?" Brooke walked up yawning and stretching her arms. "What I miss?"

"Oh how rude of you to ruin my miserable and tell me I'm beautiful. 'Cause I wasn't lookin' for love." – Alessia Cara, "I'm Yours"

#18

By the time Chyna got to Carlos' crib it was almost 3:00a.m. It took her and Brooke an hour just to calm Selena down. They had to make sure she wasn't on suicide watch before they left her alone. Finding out that your husband was bisexual and sleeping with a man behind your back would send any woman to her deathbed.

Hell, Chyna was a little fucked up behind the news herself. She'd slept with Waymon too. She'd been a fool and dropped her drawz for a man that liked dick just as much as she did. Knowing she'd slept with a gay man made Chyna wonder if she'd slept with anyone else that liked men.

Being as quiet as she could, she tiptoed into Carlos' bedroom. He lay on his side sound asleep. He looked so cute. Chyna's heart filled with love as she slipped off her clothes. Carlos liked for her to be naked when she slept with him. She loved when they lie skin-to-skin. Chyna pulled the covers back and slipped into bed next to him.

His skin smelled like Irish Spring soap. Chyna slid her arm under his and held him close. Her boobs were pressed up against his muscular back.

"Don't ever make me wait that long for you," he mumbled.

Surprised that he was awake, Chyna grinned.

"I missed you," Carlos confessed.

Time stood still. Chyna couldn't believe he'd finally said it back to her. A huge smile spread across her face. She'd never been so happy in her life.

"You can stop smiling now. Go to bed," he chuckled.

Chyna giddily kissed his shoulder blade repeatedly and did as she was told.

The smell of brown sugar bacon wafted through the air and teased Chyna's nostrils causing her to stir in her sleep. Her stomach growled as she rose from her slumber.

Chyna rubbed her eyes and stretched. The fragrant smell of bacon made her mouth water. Starving, she planted her feet on the wooden floor and headed towards the kitchen.

Sunlight cascaded over the room giving the space a golden glow. Carlos stood at the stove scrambling eggs. Seeing him at the stove whipping up a huge breakfast was like a scene out of a rom-com. He wore nothing but a pair of plaid pajama bottoms. The pajama bottoms hung low off his waist. Carlos was vibing out to the melancholy sound of Emily King. He'd prepared eggs, bacon, potatoes and cinnamon pancakes.

Chyna hadn't felt this special ever in life. For so many years she was made to feel like an afterthought. Tyreik rarely did anything special for her. She was always the one doing sweet and romantic stuff for him. He never made her feel appreciated. With him she felt like a nuisance. With Carlos nothing was hard. She didn't have to fight for his affection or attention.

He always made her feel important. He let it be known that he always wanted her around. With Tyreik, she didn't even feel comfortable enough to give him a hug. He always pushed her way. Carlos welcomed her advances. He made her feel like she was an important factor in his life. If he wasn't trying to make her fall in love with him, he was failing miserably at it.

She wished she had the words to express how she was feeling. It was beyond rude of him to make her fall for him. She'd gotten used to being miserable. Loving him wasn't what she prayed for. She'd had her heart broken before and rebuilt it with iron. But here Carlos was tearing down her walls and altering her route.

Chyna was used to men using her, so for him to be the angel he was made no sense. She didn't think men like him existed for real. She'd wrote about them in her books, but in reality, a good man was nothing but a mythical creature. Chyna wasn't a fan of love. She liked being alone. Being alone meant no one could hurt her. But Carlos made her hope for more. Chyna skipped over to him and hugged him from behind. Carlos grabbed her wrist and kissed the palm of her hand.

"Good morning, sleepyhead."

"Morning." Chyna kissed his back.

"What you do last night?"

"Oh my God." Chyna threw her hands up in the air. "You will never guess what happened." She said taking a seat at the kitchen island.

With a ton of animation, she told him the story of her late night escapade with Selena and Brooke.

"What the fuck?" Carlos chuckled as they ate breakfast. "That's crazy."

"Tell me about it. I feel so bad for Selena. I don't know how it happened but we've become friends. She's like my naïve, little, Puerto Rican sister."

"You're being really nice to her. Let me find out you have a heart," Carlos winked his eye.

"Don't worry, I'm still the Tin Man," she smirked. "You know you told me you missed me last night?"

"I know what I said," Carlos swallowed the last of his orange juice.

"So you weren't talkin' in your sleep?"

"No, I wasn't," he laughed.

"Good, I would hate to have to kick your ass," she warned, tickling his side.

"I'm not worried about it." Carlos placed another pancake onto his plate.

"Ooooh... I'll be right back." Chyna jumped up and ran to the bedroom.

She grabbed her phone from off the nightstand and rejoined Carlos at the kitchen island.

"I was so busy dealing with Selena's real-life telenovela that I didn't even check to see how many views my video got."

"What video?"

"My YouTube video."

"Are your Power reviews still doing good?"

"Really good." Chyna clicked on the video. "OMG! Look at Blue Ivy! Won't she do it? This week's video is up to thirteen thousand views already. It hasn't even been twenty-four hours."

"That's what's up. I'm proud of you." Carlos massaged her knee.

"Thank you." Chyna relished the feel of his hand. "I'm so happy. I work really hard on these videos and to see the feedback I'm getting is dope. Like, I'm so appreciative. I've been on YouTube now for almost two and a half years and I have never gotten this many views on any of my series. I've been working my ass off and it's finally starting to pay off."

"You deserve it, pretty face."

"Thank you," Chyna blushed, exposing her dimples.

"How is the book coming or is it still not coming?"

"It's not and I'm under the gun. I have to start writing soon but the words aren't coming to me," Chyna sighed taking a bite of her food.

"It's like with every book it gets harder and harder. I'm just not into it anymore. I wanna write for television and film. I want it so bad I can taste it. Like, my dream would be to write for Power. The show creator and writer,

Courtney Kemp Agboh, is a genius. I would love to work with her and have her mentor me."

"Well, you've put it out into the universe so it'll happen. You know the Bible says when two or more people come together in His name that prayers will be heard. So let's pray." Carlos took her hand and bowed his head.

Chyna bowed her head as well.

"Lord, I come to you now on this Sunday morning giving thanks to you for allowing us to see another day. Lord, you are an awesome God. You are a mighty God and sometimes I don't always understand why you allow certain things to happen but I still praise your name," Carlos prayed.

Chyna opened one eye and looked at him. She wondered what he was referring to.

"Lord, I ask that you bless Chyna with the desires of her heart. Give her discernment and lead her in the right direction. Give her clarity, God. Give her the strength and wisdom she so desperately needs. Give her the words she needs to write her book. When it comes out, let it be another best-seller. Touch Courtney Kemp's heart, God. Let her watch one of Chyna's reviews. Let her see what the world and I see. Let her see how smart, talented, and funny Chyna is so that this time next year she will be flying her out to work on the show. In Jesus' name I pray; amen." Carlos lifted his head.

"Thank you," Chyna wiped a tear from the corner of her eye.

She wanted to believe that God would hear her cries and answer her prayers but Chyna just couldn't get her hopes up. She'd been disappointed so many times in her life that she didn't get her hopes up about much anymore. Chyna learned to savor each day and what it brought. She never tried to look too far in the future.

Her life never went as she planned. All she knew for sure was that she was unbelievably happy that Sunday morning. The way Carlos looked at her while she told him her hopes and dreams made her believe anything was possible. Carlos saw for the first time optimism in her eyes. From the first day he saw her, all he saw was confusion and uncertainty. He enjoyed seeing her so carefree and relaxed. He wanted every day for her to be that way.

"Come here." He held her hand.

Chyna rose to her feet and followed him to the middle of the kitchen floor. Emily King's *U & I* played as he wrapped her up in his embrace. Chyna's small frame fit perfectly in his arms. He wished she knew how much he cared for her. The more time he spent with her, the harder he fell. He missed her whenever she was gone. Love was beginning to bloom in his heart but he couldn't tell her that.

Love and Carlos didn't mix. It failed him every time. Anytime he tried to feel for someone else, nothing but negativity entered the picture. Carlos couldn't love Chyna 'cause if he loved her, he'd hurt her. His heart wasn't ready to take that leap. Love did him dirty. He and Bellamy were supposed to have the perfect little family but here he was alive and well while his baby boy lay six feet deep.

Life wasn't fair and Carlos no longer believed in happy endings. There was no future for him and Chyna. All he could do was enjoy her while she swayed to the beat in his arms. All he had to offer was today. Anything beyond

that would be a lie.

"Already replaced you with a new girl." – Tank feat. Chris Brown, "Lonely"

#19

Chyna danced around her living room like a little kid on Christmas morning. Life hadn't been this good in a long while. Everything was falling in place. She hadn't expected to fall so hard for Carlos but she welcomed the notion. He made her heart sing and it seemed like he felt the same way. The more time they spent together, the more he opened up. Carlos was very mysterious. He didn't reveal too much about himself.

At first Chyna didn't care because she hadn't planned on getting so involved with him. But now she yearned to know as much about him as possible. She knew what made him tick but she wanted to know what made his heart beat, what made him want to get up in the morning. Did she do it for him? Did he see a future with her?

She saw him being in her life forever. She envisioned him being a part of her and India's little family. He would be a great addition to their party of two. She never thought after having her heart carved out of her chest with a knife by Tyreik that she'd have room to love another. But Carlos made her feel like loving someone without being hurt was possible.

Maybe this time she wouldn't be cast aside. Maybe, just maybe, Carlos would stay around for the long haul. Maybe Chyna would have her happily ever after, after all. After everything she'd been through, she deserved nothing less. As she twirled around on her tippy toes like a ballerina, the sound of her phone ringing sidetracked her dance moves. It was India calling. Chyna raced over to the phone. She hadn't talked to her baby girl in two days.

"Hello?" She panted out of breath.

"What you doing? Why you sound like that?" India quizzed hoping her mother wasn't doing the nasty.

"I was cleaning up the kitchen," Chyna lied.

Her daughter didn't need to know that she was over there acting like a Disney princess behind a man.

"How was Paris? Did you go to the Louvre?"

"Mama, it was so dope. We got to see the Mona Lisa and the Venus De Milo. It was so cool," India gushed.

"I wish I could be there with you so we could've experienced it together." Chyna poked out her bottom lip, disappointed.

"Maybe we can come back. Just me and you," India suggested.

"I might have to make that happen. You haven't had any problems have you?" Chyna asked, worried.

She could hear a hint of sadness in her daughter's voice.

"No, I'm just a little homesick, that's all."

"If you wanna come home early and spend the rest of the summer with me you can," Chyna tried to persuade her.

She missed India terribly. It was almost sickening how much. India was her rib, her best friend. They'd grown up together. Chyna didn't remember a day where her daughter wasn't by her side. She made Chyna feel whole. Not having her around felt like a piece of her soul was missing.

"I'm ok. I'ma stick it out. I can't miss out on going to Madrid and Barcelona."

"You sure?" Chyna questioned unsure.

"Yeah, I'm sure. Before you know it summer will be over and I'll be back home bugging you," India laughed.

"Tell me about it," Chyna laughed as there was a knock on the door. "Baby, there's somebody at the door."

"Go ahead and answer it."

"I'ma call you later to check on you. Answer the phone, Indy," Chyna spoke sternly.

"I will, Mom," India groaned, rolling her eyes.

"Roll your eyes again and see what happen," Chyna warned like a mother.

She knew her daughter all too well.

"Bye, Mom," India giggled.

"Bye, my baby, and be safe." Chyna ended the call and raced down the steps.

Unsure of who it was, she peeked out the blinds. Selena and Delicious waved back at her like two Jehova Witnesses.

"You have got to be kidding me." She unlocked the door shocked and bewildered. "Now both of y'all are stalking me?" Chyna placed her hand on her hip.

"Ju know ju missed me," Selena air-kissed her cheek.

"And we brought you food." Delicious held up a takeout bag from Miso. "Selena told me how much you like to eat."

"The only reason I'm letting y'all in is 'cause y'all brought me food." Chyna stepped to the side. "But don't make this no habit."

"This li'l Cruella de Vil act you got going on is not believable," Delicious sashayed past her.

"Who asked you, RuPaul? You betta shut up before I make you and Penelope Cruz sashay away." Chyna locked the door behind them. "So y'all have made it official? Y'all sister wives now?"

"We real good Judies now," Delicious stated, walking up the steps.

"I don't no who dis Judy person is but jes we are friends." Selena sat at Chyna's dining room table.

"Selena, you are one crazy chick. Who befriends their husband's mistress?"

"He didn't no so why wouldn't I be his friend? Waymon is the dirty mule. He was the one playing the both of us."

"Sure was; but in the end, he played himself," Delicious popped his lips.

"So what happened after everything went down the other night?" Chyna dug into her food.

"He tried to make me believe that hem and Delicious was a one-time thing but I'm no i-d-iot." Selena waved her index finger. "I told hem I wanted a divorce and put hem out."

"Good girl." Chyna gave her a high-five.

"After she put him out that fool had the nerve to call me and ask if he could come stay with me," Delicious exclaimed. "Chile, I cussed that nigga out so good I had to go repent and pray."

"Hell naw," Chyna laughed. "So what now? Are you going to stay here in St. Louis or move back to Miami?" She asked Selena.

"After my cou-zins wedding I'm going back to Mi-ami. I need to be around my family. I need their support."

"I think that's a good idea."

"Now speaking of my cou-zins wedding." Selena glanced over at Delicious then back at Chyna. "I want ju to come to her wedding with us."

"Excuse you?" Chyna raised her brow.

"My cou-zins wedding is tomorrow and I don't no anybody there but her. I want ju and Delicious to come so I won't be lonely," Selena pleaded.

"I'm so sick of yo' begging-ass I don't know what to do!" Chyna dropped her chopsticks in a huff. "You just gon' make me be your friend?"

"Ju are my friend." Selena reached over and hugged her.

Chyna grumbled, rolling her eyes. She couldn't front, Selena's worrisome-ass was her homegirl. She'd grown fond of her. She didn't have anything planned the next day, so hitting up a wedding wouldn't be so bad.

"Is there an open bar?"

"Jes," Selena smiled from ear to ear.

"Bet, I'm in."

It had been years since Chyna had gone to a wedding. The last one had been Asia and Jaylen's. She hoped that the next wedding she attended would be her own but that wasn't the case. Marriage wasn't anywhere on her radar. She'd just started to get comfortable with the thought of being in a relationship again.

Selena's cousin's wedding was stunning nonetheless. As soon as Chyna walked into the ceremony space she felt as if she had been transported into a mystical wonderland. Shades of cream and soft pink filled the room. Behind the alter was a huge bay window. Real cherry blossom trees and candles lined the white runner down the aisle. Vintage, wooden pews were on each side of the room for the guest to sit.

Chyna and the bride had similar taste. The color palette and choice of decorations were the same as what she would've chosen. Selena's cousin had exceptional taste. Chyna couldn't wait to meet her and see her gown. It was a black tie wedding so everyone in attendance was dressed in their Sunday's Best. Selena looked exquisite in a gold trumpet gown. The gown accentuated her full breast and curvaceous hips.

Delicious wore a fabulous, black, Tom Ford suit. The suit fit him impeccably well. It was tailor-made to show off his toned and taut ass. The gag was he wore no shirt underneath. Homeboy came bare-chested like a muthafucka. Delicious was definitely trying to catch some trade.

Chyna wasn't mad at him. There was no point in crying over spilled milk. When one man fucked up, her philosophy was to get under a new one. If she wasn't madly in love with Carlos she would've gotten on a few of the eligible bachelors in the room. She'd noticed a few girls from the old neighborhood at the wedding. They kept looking back at her and whispering. Chyna started to think she had something on her face but that couldn't be.

She knew she was beat to the gods. Chyna pulled out her Chanel compact and examined her face and teeth. The black smoky eye and nude lip she rocked was intact. There wasn't anything in her teeth. *Them ho's just hating. I look good*, she thought, closing the compact mirror. Chyna shut it down as soon as she walked through the door.

Her hair was parted down the middle and slicked down. She wore no jewelry. Her dress was her statement piece. She rocked a black, lace, Alexandre Vauthier dress. The dress had a halter neckline and a thigh-high split. A pair of black, strappy, Alaïa heels made her toned legs look long and lean. Chyna was showing major skin. He arms, back and legs were all out for everyone to see. She wasn't wearing white but Chyna was giving the bride a run for her money. After the ceremony, she couldn't wait to run over to Carlos' place so he could see how good she looked.

"Why them ho's keep looking at you? We got beef in this muthafucka?" Delicious asked, ready to set it off.

"Shit, that's what I'm trying to figure out." Chyna mean-mugged the girls.

"Selena, let me find out you set me up to get jumped 'cause I fucked yo' husband." Chyna glared at her.

"I don't no those girls." Selena replied honestly.

"I ain't come prepared to fight but please believe one of these hoes will get knocked the fuck out." Chyna confirmed down for whatever.

Thankfully for everyone in attendance the wedding began and she didn't have to get rowdy. Everyone except Chyna clapped as the pastor and the groom came out. Time and space stood still. Her limbs wouldn't budge. Tears flooded the brim of her brown eyes. *This can't be happening*, she thought. Her worst nightmare was coming true. What had she done to deserve this?

"Chyna, what's wrong?" Delicious asked.

She was shaking so bad her heels clattered against the floor.

"Did you know?" She asked Selena.

"No what?" Selena asked seeing how distraught she was.

Chyna was a mess. She could barely think straight.

"Did you know?" She yelled.

The people in front of them turned around to see what the commotion was.

"What are ju talking about, mami?"

Not getting the answers she needed, Chyna focused her attention back on the groom. He was staring right at her. Chyna's bottom lip quivered as what seemed like a million tears streamed down her face. Tyreik stared at her with contempt in his eyes. He had no idea what she was doing there.

Hot lava simmered in the pit of Chyna's stomach as she realized she was at Tyreik's wedding. He stood a few feet away from her about to marry someone else. They'd been together since she was sixteen and he never thought enough of her to make her his wife. The conversation of marriage was always brushed off.

He made her feel like she wasn't marriage material. For years he played around with her love when she did nothing but hold him down. It hadn't even been two years and he was about to marry someone else. Here she was stressing and feeling guilty over the accident and he was chilling. She wondered constantly about his well-being. She didn't know if he'd gotten his health back or not.

All of those questions were answered. She watched his smug-ass stand at the alter in a black, Gucci, emerald pattern tuxedo awaiting his bride. The nigga was doing quite well. He looked better than ever. He wasn't as buff as he once was. He'd slimmed down a bit but his mocha skin still called her name. Tyreik still had the same menacing glare in his eye that drew her to him at sixteen.

Chyna always thought if she saw him at the alter she'd be the one greeting him at the end. But no, she was a guest at his nuptials. The universe had to be playing a cruel joke on her. This was some foul shit. Chyna had to get out of there. At any second she was going to vomit or start throwing hands. The only problem was, the wedding march had begun to play. The bride was on her way out.

"I gotta get out of here!" She cringed as the piano keys rang in her ear.

"Mami, what's wrong?" Selena panicked.

She was worried that Chyna was having a heart attack.

"Get me out of here! Get me out of here! Get me out of here!" Chyna screeched, stomping her feet as the doors opened.

Everyone rose to their feet. Selena's cousin Loupita and her father linked arms and proceeded down the aisle. Chyna looked at Tyreik then back at his bride. She wore a cathedral veil and a Reem Acra ball gown. Unlike Selena, Loupita wasn't as beautiful. She was alright looking. At best, she was a basic beauty. If Chyna saw her out she wouldn't look at her twice.

"I gotta go!" She grabbed her Judith Leiber clutch and bogarted her way past the people in her pew.

She didn't care that she stepped on a few toes or the fact that everyone was eyeing her instead of the bride. She had to get out of there before she had a stroke. Chyna was moving so fast that the hem of her dress got caught in her shoe causing her to fall. Chyna fell face first into the middle of the aisle. Everyone gasped in horror. To make matters worse, she landed right in front of the bride and her father.

Chyna had never been so embarrassed in her life. She lie on the floor before the bride's feet. Chyna wanted to curl up in a ball and die. She was mortified and her knee was bruised. Chyna would've gladly taken her last breath right then and there. Instead, she sprang to her feet and looked back at Tyreik. He shot her a look of disgust and pity.

He didn't give a fuck about her. Nothing about him had changed. He was still the same old, self-centered, unsympathetic muthafucka he was when he was with her. Cursing the day she ever laid eyes on him, Chyna gathered the bottom of her dress and dashed past the bride. If she ever saw Tyreik's face again it would be too soon.

"I stand accused of fuckboy behavior."

– Tank, "So Cold"

#20

Run! Don't stop, Chyna told herself as the wind swept against her face. She didn't know exactly where she was running to but she couldn't stop her feet from moving. She was blocks away from the venue but she still wasn't far enough. She had to escape the madness that surrounded her. When the ache in Chyna's feet took over her will to run off the face of the earth, she stopped.

Completely out of breath, she placed her hand on her knees and wheezed. Her feet were sure to have blisters on them later. Running like Usain Bolt in five inch heels was not the move. Standing up straight, she leaned up against a brick wall. She had a small amount of blood on her hand from the bruise on her knee. Selena and Delicious were blowing up her phone but Chyna didn't have the strength or energy to talk to them. She needed her day one friends.

Chyna caught her breath and pulled out her phone to call Brooke. To her dismay, she didn't pick up. Heated, she called Asia. Two phone calls later, Asia didn't answer either. Chyna hated when some major shit was going down and her friends were nowhere to be found. The only other person she felt comfortable enough to turn to was Carlos. He would understand her despair. Chyna dialed his number. Furious was not the word to describe how mad she was when he didn't pick up the phone either.

Beyond annoyed, she called an Uber to come pick her up. Since Carlos wouldn't answer, she was going to stop by his place and talk to him in person instead. On the way over she called him several more times and still didn't get a response. Chyna was distraught. She needed comforting. She wanted nothing more than to run into his arms and cry a gallon of gasoline tears.

She felt stupid as hell. She'd given Tyreik more years than he ever deserved and here he was marrying some chick he'd known for five minutes. He acted like what they shared never existed. How could he so easily vow to give his heart to someone else and not deal with their baggage first? The two of them still had so much left on the table that needed to be said.

Chyna no longer wanted him to be her man or her husband. She'd already come to the realization that her and Tyreik were never meant to be. Loving him taught her that she deserved to have a man love her wholeheartedly. She didn't need a part-time, sometime lover. Chyna deserved the sun, moon and the stars.

She didn't need a man in her life who constantly disrespected her and made her feel less than what she was. She didn't deserve to be emotionally abused. What she deserved was a man that was emotionally available. The only thing she wanted was for him to apologize for the hell he took her through. Had he forgotten all the times he'd made her cry, the times he tore her down, broke her spirit, all the lies, broken promises and the times he'd cheated?

How was he so in love with another woman after only a year and a half? What did the Puerto Rican Princess have that Chyna didn't? Was she more subservient and easier to get along with? Did she turn a blind eye to his lies or had he done a drastic 180 after the accident and completely changed? Chyna had so many questions that needed to be answered but first she needed to see her baby. The Uber pulled in front of Carlos' house and parked.

Chyna turned up her face and got out of the car. Carlos' car was parked out front of his house. He was at home so she didn't understand why he wasn't answering the phone. *Maybe he's asleep,* she thought using her key to unlock the door. The loud sound of Jay Z's *Party Life* and the smell of weed hit her as soon as she walked in. *Well he's not sleep,* she thought walking further inside.

A sick feeling washed over her body. Something wasn't right. Chyna rounded the corner and stopped dead in her tracks. She found Carlos sitting on the couch with some Cara Delevingne looking bitch. They were sipping wine and having a grand old time. The chick had her shoes off and was curled up on the couch. It was obvious this wasn't her first time there. Homegirl was mad comfortable.

Carlos didn't even have on a shirt. He was maxing and relaxing in a pair of hooping shorts with a freshly-fucked look on his face. *Did he just fuck this bitch,* Chyna wondered. She felt as if she'd been kicked in the stomach twice in one day. *So that's why this nigga didn't answer the phone. He in here wit' another bitch,* she fumed in disbelief.

"Oh word?" She yelled getting his attention.

Carlos looked up at her surprised. The girl he was with gazed over her shoulder stunned as well.

"What you doing here?" He asked turning the music down.

"So this what we do now? You just gon' have some random bitch over here knowing I got a goddamn key?" Chyna threw it at him. "I'm so sick of you trifling-ass niggas I don't know what to do! All you muthafuckas is the same! All y'all do is lie and play games! You ain't have to sell me no goddamn dream, Carlos! You could've fucked me for free! But you a fuckboy just like the rest of these niggas! Check this out though. Let me tell you something," she inched closer to him to make her point clear.

"You got me fucked up. You think you about to play me for a fool? Shiiiit... baby girl, you can have 'em. A bitch like me ain't never pressed for no dick." She spat before walking out and leaving them behind with a startled expression on their faces.

Chyna hadn't even been home a good twenty minutes when she heard the sound of Carlos' fist pounding on the door. She stood frozen stiff wondering if she should even bother to answer it. He had a key; if he wanted to get in so bad he would use it or had he forgotten she'd given him one? Chyna had nothing to say to him. She didn't want to hear anything he said either. As far as she was concerned, he could save his tired-ass explanation. With her arms folded across her chest, she tapped her heel against the hardwood floor.

"I ain't answering shit. His ass gon' be knocking till his hands get sore." She looked down and admired her nails.

Chyna pursed her lips and paced back and forth across the living room floor. The train of her dress glided behind her like a cape. She was so upset that her entire body shook. It was ironic how the two men she ever gave a damn about played her less than an hour apart of each other. After the day Chyna had, she was officially done giving a fuck. When she didn't allow herself to feel, life was far less complicated. Giving zero fucks was the way to live. But Carlos wouldn't allow her to go about her day in peace. He was now banging on the door and ringing the bell at the same time while screaming her name.

"Chyna, I know you're in there! Open the fuckin' door!" He barked like a maniac.

Chyna squeezed her eyes shut and tried to wish him away. She wanted to fucking disappear. She didn't want to deal with Carlos and his shit. If she did, she was sure to lose what little religion she had left. Carlos was determined to make her act a fool. He obviously didn't give a fuck about her neighbors. He wanted a fight so Chyna was going to give it to him. Fed up, she picked up the hem of her dress and stomped down the steps.

"What the fuck do you want? Why are you banging on my door like a fuckin' idiot?" She yelled snatching it open. "I ain't got shit to say to you! Go back and be with that bitch you had sittin' on yo' fuckin' couch!" She bobbed her head.

"Shut the fuck up!" Carlos stormed inside and grabbed her by the arm.

"You better let me go!" Chyna looked at him like he was crazy.

"Chyna." Carlos spun around and shot her a venomous glance. "I'm warning you. Shut the fuck up."

Chyna didn't know why but she did as she was told. The deranged glimmer in his eyes had her on pause. *This nigga crazy*, she thought. Seeing that he'd made his point, Carlos resumed dragging her up the stairs by her arm. Chyna followed behind him trying her best to keep up. She was determined not to fall. Carlos still had her by the crook of her arm as they made their way into the living room. Heated, he pushed her down onto the couch. Chyna fell back with a thump. She'd never seen Carlos so furious. His face burned a devil red.

"You got a lot of fuckin' nerve coming up this muthafucka like you're the one with the attitude!" She snapped.

"Yo, I knew I shouldn't have fucked wit' you! You're fuckin' crazy. You come up in my spot accusing me of some shit I ain't even on, like you my fuckin' girlfriend! We ain't together! I don't owe you shit! If I did have another chick up in my shit that I was fuckin' wit', I can do that. But that was my fuckin' sister! You really think I'ma give you a key to my crib then have another bitch up in there knowing damn well you can stop by at any time? Come on now. You gotta think smart." He pounded his finger against his head.

Chyna sat quiet. She hadn't even thought of that. When she spotted him with the girl, the thought that she could've been a family member or friend didn't even cross her mind. Suddenly all of her anger disappeared. She felt like a complete idiot. Chyna sat up, placed her face in her hands and cried. She'd really fucked up this time.

"Yeah, you feel dumb, don't you?" Carlos shot.

Chyna gazed up at him somberly.

"I'm so sorry. I —" She tried to explain but Carlos cut her off.

"Nah, fuck that! That's the second time you've come to my spot on some dumb shit. Had my sister lookin' at me like I'm crazy. I told you the last time you came to my crib on some rah-rah shit that I don't play that. But nah, you wanna accuse me of bullshit instead of opening your mouth and talkin' to me like a fuckin' adult!"

"I'm sorry," Chyna sobbed. "You just don't understand what kind of day I've had—"

"Fuck yo' day!" Carlos shouted angrily.

He was genuinely hurt by Chyna's actions.

"You ever stop to think that I might be going through some shit too?"

Chyna didn't dare say a word.

"No, you didn't. And since you wanna act like a fuckin' brat and give me back my key, give me back the bracelets I bought you."

Chyna examined her wrist. She didn't want to give him back the Cartier LOVE bracelets he'd given her. They meant a lot to her. She knew that him giving her the bracelets was a huge step for him.

"No." She shook her head.

"Nah, you wanna act like a crazy bitch, give 'em back," Carlos demanded.

"Hold up, don't call me no bitch." Chyna's nostrils flared.

"Don't call me a nigga and I won't call you a bitch. 'Cause if I call you a nigga all hell gon' break loose." Carlos proved a point.

"You damn right it will." Chyna nodded her head.

"Exactly, so let that be the last time you call me out my fuckin' name. Try that shit with them other muthafuckas you fuck wit. I'm not your fuckin' boyfriend. We ain't like that." He reminded her.

Chyna's heart sank down to her feet. She knew she wasn't his girl but to hear him say it stung like hell. Plus, she knew she was wrong for calling him a nigga. It wasn't right. She had to stop.

"I know I'm not your girlfriend; and who said I wanted to be? You know what? Here! Take these raggedy-ass bracelets back!" She tried her best to take the bracelets off to no avail. "FUCK!" She screamed.

Carlos shot her a menacing glare.

"Don't ever give me back something I gave you unless I ask for it." He threw the key to his house onto her lap.

Unwilling to act like she gave a fuck that he'd given it back, Chyna rose to her feet. The key fell to the floor and flipped over several times before landing underneath her coffee table.

"Fuck that key. You can leave." She tried to push past him.

Carlos grabbed her and pushed her back down.

"You gon' stop trying to be so tough." He laid on top of her and made her spread her legs. "You gon' quit disrespecting me." He ran his hand up her thigh and ripped off her thong.

Chyna gasped for air. She didn't know how she and Carlos had gone from hating each other's guts to fucking each other's brains out. It was sick and sinful but felt totally right. She hated the control he had over her mind and her body. No other man could curse her out and then fuck her afterwards.

Sure, she'd overreacted and accused him of something he didn't do, but to have him remind her that she was nothing to him but a chick he fucked, hurt like hell. She didn't know how she'd ended up here. She thought they were moving towards a relationship but apparently that wasn't the case. They were in a situationship.

As he inserted his dick deep into her vaginal soul, she wondered did he even want to be with her. He'd never said it. Hell, it took him weeks just to admit he missed her. Was she only a pretty face and a good lay for him?

Carlos slowly pounded in and out of her, spellbound by the affect she had on him. It infuriated him that he allowed her to get away with the shit she did. Chyna was problematic, defensive and explosive. She was maddening but as he stroked her middle he couldn't help but notice the sadness in her eyes.

Had he been the one to cause her pain? Carlos hated to see her upset but Chyna had brought the misery she felt onto herself. She couldn't go around acting the way she did and not think there would be consequences to her actions. He wanted to be there for her to help her on the road to self-discovery but Carlos couldn't help heal anyone when he was broken himself.

Moments like this were the exact reason why he shielded his heart. Love and emotions were entirely too complicated. He didn't like feeling angry and confused. He didn't like that when he kissed her beautiful, brown skin he saw visions of his future and her one day being his wife. Dealing with Chyna was becoming too much. They were supposed to be having fun but now that love was knocking on both of their doors, everything was turning to shit. He had to let her go.

"Never mind your mistakes. Pick it up from the place we were." – Alex Isley, "My Theme"

#21

All the lights in Chyna's bedroom were off. The darkness soothed her bruised ego. The whiskey burned her throat as she drank but it gave her clarity. She needed her baby back. At the moment, she'd take Carlos however she could have him.

Almost a week had passed since they got into it. She hadn't heard from him since. She'd tried to call him several times but neither time did he bother to pick up. Chyna was completely distraught behind his silent treatment. Whenever Tyreik used to get mad at her he'd shut her out and do the same thing. It killed her.

"How could he just cut me off?" She cried taking a swig from the Jack Daniels bottle she had in her hand.

She missed him so bad it was pathetic. He used to be sweet and call her at least twice a day. She didn't know how long he planned on punishing her but she couldn't take it. He had to know how she felt about him by now. Chyna couldn't even hide it anymore. She loved him. She hadn't planned on it happening but she did. He'd awakened things in her she didn't even know existed.

But she had to know where she stood with him. Did he not want her like she wanted him? Everything with him was such a blur. Nothing with Carlos was black and white. There was always a grey area. She couldn't figure him out. He treated her like a queen but still found a way to keep her at bay. He couldn't continue to play tetherball with her heart. Either he was going to be all in or step the fuck off.

Her friends had tried calling her but Chyna only wanted Carlos. Only he could fill the void in her chest. She only wanted to reveal her thoughts and doubts to him. Seeing Tyreik had really done a number on her. She was thrown for a loop. She needed time to recuperate.

Since their breakup, Chyna hadn't been herself. She was a shell of a woman. She hadn't realized how bitter she was until Carlos re-entered her life. For a brief moment she'd begun to feel like her old self and it was all due to him. But now she'd found a way to push him away and ruin things. Anything good in her life, Chyna destroyed.

She didn't know how to accept the good things that came her way. She always felt there was bullshit behind it. She didn't even realize that she subconsciously sabotaged things with her over-the-top behavior. She wanted to change. She just didn't know how. She didn't like that it was hard for her to trust. She hated that she doubted the goodness inside of people.

She only had herself to blame. Staying with Tyreik all those years had wrecked her. He'd torn her to shreds. When she saw him standing at the alter, all she could do was remember all the chicks he'd cheated on her with and the abuse. He'd left her emotionally cripple. Now that she'd found Carlos she thought that he'd be the man to resurrect her dreams. But instead, here she was alone drowning her sorrows with brown liquor.

Memories of the way he touched her made her cry. She missed the way he quieted her fears with a simple kiss on the lips. Chyna had to make him see how sorry she was. She would never react so brashly again. She'd learned her lesson. Taking a huge gulp of Jack, she hit the blunt she had lit and grabbed her phone. She couldn't take another minute of despair.

She was sick of fist fighting with her emotions. She was sloppy drunk and high out of her mind but none of that mattered. She had to show him how much pain she was in. She was tired of him withholding his love from her. It was time he admitted that he was madly in love with her too. Chyna held the phone up to her ear.

By the fourth ring she knew he wasn't going to pick up. Her fingers trembled as she placed the blunt up to her lips. With each ring she felt like she was falling apart. After six rings his voicemail kicked in. Chyna normally didn't leave voicemail messages but she thought if he heard the sound of her voice he'd soften up. At the sound of the beep she rocked back and forth.

"What do I have to do to get inside your muthafuckin' heart? Huh? I said I was sorry for the other day. You gotta forgive me 'cause... I'm no good without you." She laid her heart out on the line.

The whiskey had her feeling pretty and somehow had become an unwanted truth serum.

"I need you here with me. You know I can't sleep at night unless you're by my side. And," Chyna took the phone away from her ear and checked the time." I know it's four in the morning but come over and have a drink with me. Let's stay up late and smoke a J and work this shit out. Just... please don't leave me. Call me back." She held her breath.

Tears filled the back of her throat. She'd never been so emotionally naked in years. She'd perfected being unaffected, so to now open her heart was like ripping off a Band-Aid. Taking the risk of being rejected wasn't something Chyna took lightly. If Carlos didn't respond back she was sure to shatter into a million pieces.

Drops of rain tap danced against Carlos' umbrella. The sky that Wednesday morning was grey and cloudy. A cool breeze swept through the air. It was unusually cold for it to only be July 22nd. The gloomy weather perfectly reflected his mood. With his hand in his jean pocket, he shuffled from one foot to another. Mud squished under the soles of his shoes. He wanted to look up at his son's headstone but his eyes couldn't bare the sight.

Carlos was a strong man but dealing with the death of his newborn boy had taken the fight out of him. He hadn't come to terms with the fact that the God he prayed to each day and night could be the same God that took his son away. The God he served could never be so cruel. It had been a year since his baby boy passed. Carlos thought of him every day.

When Bellamy became pregnant he wasn't sure of them starting a family at first. He and Bellamy had just gotten back together. He was still hung up on Chyna and reconciling with the fact that she had abruptly ended their budding love affair. His head was all over the place. He didn't really know what to think or feel at the time. He loved Bellamy a lot but thoughts of what him and Chyna could've been plagued him.

He hated that she could so easily cut him off. There was no explanation. She simply stopped taking his calls. Fast forward a little over a year and half later, and here he was doing the same exact thing to her. He'd heard her tearful plea on his voicemail but Carlos couldn't get past all the things she'd said and done. He missed her too but had no room for drama. He was already dealing with enough.

His baby lay under his feet lifeless. When she came over that day acting crazy, he was having a conversation with his sister about the one-year anniversary of his son's death. Carlos wasn't emotionally ready to handle the day. The wound was still fresh and sore.

After getting over the initial shock of Bellamy's pregnancy, he settled into the idea of him finally being a dad. Carlos had always wanted a family. He and Bellamy had tried for years. They suffered heartache after heartache when their attempts failed. From the moment he met her, he saw her being the mother of his kids.

Bellamy was one hell of a woman. She was smart, successful and caring. She was his high school sweetheart. He'd move heaven and earth for her. She'd loved him when he had nothing. She loved him before the fancy cars and iced out jewels. She'd been his rock during the difficult times the world brought his way. He was destroyed when she left him.

He was in it for the long haul. He never wanted a divorce. But he didn't want to be the source of her discomfort. After the death of Dash, she hated the sight of him. He knew she was only acting out because of her postpartum. He was willing to give her the time she needed to heal but Bellamy wanted him gone. Carlos hated that after their second go-round they'd ended up separate once again.

"I think of you every day, li'l man." His voice cracked.

"I didn't know you would be here?" Carlos heard a familiar voice say from behind.

Bellamy walked over and stood by his side. Carlos choked back his tears and looked at her. She was crying as well. Grief was written all over her face. She missed their son just as much as he did. Even through the pain she still looked as beautiful as she did when they were seventeen.

Quietly, he took her hand in his. Neither of them said a word. They just stood and let their grief consume them. Thoughts of what their son could've been filled their heads. Carlos hated God for what he'd done.

He craved structure. He was tired of hurting. He missed the familiarity of having Bellamy around. He despised the fact that loving Chyna wasn't something he could shake. His emotions were all over the place. He hated not being in control. He needed to pick up the pieces of his life. Bellamy eyed him with sorrow in her eyes.

"I know you've moved on and if we never speak to each other after this, I'll understand. But I love you and I miss you. I want you to come home. I'm sorry for the way I acted. I shouldn't have pushed you away but I wasn't myself. I just want you back. I want our family back. We can't let what happened to Dash destroy what we had. You and I are meant to be together. I know you believe that."

Carlos stared deep into her soul. At one point Bellamy was his best friend and his soulmate. He couldn't see past her. A part of him still thought they had a future but then there was Chyna. He loved her but he and Bellamy still had so much more that needed to be explored. He was still getting to know Chyna. He couldn't dive in head first knowing a piece of him still belonged to another woman. It wouldn't be fair to her. He didn't want to do her like that.

"Can we go somewhere and talk?" Bellamy begged with her eyes. "Please… just give me a minute to explain myself."

"A'ight."

"Don't take it personal. I just can't give you what you want." – Keke Palmer, "I Don't Belong To You"

#22

Bar Louie was poppin'. Everybody was out for drinks, food and a good time but Chyna couldn't have fun if she tried. She sat amongst her friends shoving her food back and forth across her plate. The chicken pasta she ordered wasn't appetizing at all. She'd barely been able to eat a thing. Having no communication with Carlos was driving her insane. She wanted to reach out again but couldn't risk playing herself any more than she already had.

The morning after she drunk dialed him she regretted every word. Chyna wasn't in the business of begging for attention, especially not from a man. There were plenty of dudes dying to get with her. But no, here she was stuck on a sexy-ass white boy that obviously wasn't checkin' for her. He'd moved on as if what they shared never existed.

For Chyna, every minute they spent together would forever be embedded in her memory. Now those memories had become cancerous. She'd fallen ill because of his negligence. This was not how she saw this playing out. She thought she'd have her way with him and keep it moving like she'd done the rest. Never did she think she'd be sprung behind a man. A white man no less.

You should've never looked in his eyes, she thought running her hands through her hair. Chyna gazed up at her friends. They were all looking at her like she was crazy. Brooke, Delicious and Selena were all worried about her well-being. Chyna hadn't cracked a smile or a joke all day. She hadn't even touched her food. Baby girl had it bad.

Somehow she'd managed to come out the house looking decent. She wore a pair of aviator shades, a blue jean button-up with the sleeves rolled up, skin-tight, denim, skinny legs that hit right above her ankle and nude, pointed-toe Manolo Blahnik heels. Her look was simple but chic as hell. The first four buttons of her shirt were unbuttoned to show off her ample cleavage. Mad dudes tried to catch her attention but Chyna was off in her world. She wasn't thinking about none of them dudes.

"If this what fuckin' a white man do to you, then I don't ever want no white meat. I'ma stick to dark meat," Delicious clarified shaking his head.

"You got that right," Brooke gave him a high-five.

"He got her over here missing meals and shit. Uh ah, I don't want no dick like that," Delicious pledged. "Carlos got that Future dick. That's some old voodoo penis. Don't nobody want no voodoo dick."

"Ju ok, friend?" Selena wrapped her arm around Chyna's shoulder. "Ju no I'm gonna miss ju when I leave next week."

"I'ma miss yo' crazy-ass too." Chyna patted her hand. "How was the wedding after I left?"

"My cou-zin cried the whole time. She was a wreck. She cried during the ceremony and the reception. She was so mad that ju messed up her wed-ding."

"I feel bad... for her... kinda sorta... but not him though," Chyna said unsure of her feelings.

"Her husss-band attacked me with a bunch of questions. He was very angry. He asked me if I brought ju to be malicious and if ju were jealous that he was getting married to someone else. I explained to hem that ju had no idea that it was his wed-ding. I don't think he believed me but whatever." Selena flicked her wrist.

"The hell wit' Tyreik. Ain't nobody thinkin' about him," Chyna responded dryly.

She honestly didn't give a fuck how he felt. The fact that Chyna didn't have the energy to talk shit about Tyreik alarmed Brooke.

"You want me to buy you a drink? Will that make you feel better?" She poked out her bottom lip.

"Nah, I'ma lay off the booze for a while." Chyna pushed her plate away.

"Oh hell naw! It's worse than I thought!" Brooke said truly worried about her best friend.

"Y'all know I'm a part of the PPG. We can get this muthafucka poppin'. Get that nigga jumped. Just say the word and a bitch will make it happen." Delicious declared, snapping his finger.

"What is the PPG?" Chyna eyed him confused.

"The Pink Pussy Gang. We meet up on Tuesdays and Thursdays."

"I'm not about to play with you," Chyna replied unwilling to laugh.

"I don't know what I'ma do, y'all." She hung her head back in despair. "He got me shook and I don't know what to do."

"Call hem," Selena suggested placing Chyna's phone in her hand.

"That ain't happening." Chyna placed her phone back on the table. "If he wanna talk to me he'll call." She assured as her phone started to ring.

The sound startled her and the girls.

"Oh my God. It's him." Chyna announced astonished.

"Answer it, fool!" Brooke urged.

Chyna was nervous as fuck as she answered the call.

"Hello?" She answered trying to sound as nonchalant as possible.

She couldn't let on that she'd been on suicide watch for the past week. That was nobody's business but hers and God's.

"What you doing?" Carlos asked.

His deep voice sent chills up Chyna's spine. *Damn I miss this muthafucka*, her heart skipped a beat.

"At Bar Louie having lunch with my friends. Why, what's up?"

"You got a minute? I'ma swing by and come get you."

Chyna's heart rate increased. This was what she'd been waiting for. She'd finally get to see him so they could squash their beef.

"That's cool," she replied coolly.

"A'ight, I'll see you in a minute." Carlos hung up.

Chyna ended the call and smiled brightly.

"He's about to come get me," she shrilled.

"Hallelujah!" Brooke put her hands up in the air. "Look at Blue Ivy! Won't she do it?"

"Who is dis Blue Ivy ju all speak of?" Selena asked thoroughly confused.

"Selena, don't make me slap you," Chyna cautioned.

She did not play when it came to Blue Ivy Carter.

"Right," Brooke looked her up-and-down. "I rebuke you, devil, in the name of Jesus. You will not disrespect Blue."

Chyna pulled out her compact mirror and examined her face. She had to make sure she was on point when she saw Carlos. She was straight. Minutes later he pulled up in front of the restaurant in his black, old school, Buick Skylark. The car was clean as hell. The jet black paint glistened under the beam of the afternoon sun.

Chyna said goodbye to her friends and switched over to his car. Carlos watched as she strutted over to him. He knew that seeing her in person was a bad idea. Chyna wasn't the type of woman you could look past. Her beauty consumed you. Her hips swayed from side-to-side as if she was doing the merengue.

It was hard to pretend that they were just friends when visions of him having her pent down while hitting her from behind flooded his brain. Carlos leaned over and unlocked the passenger door for her to get in. Chyna climbed inside. The hypnotic smell of his cologne engulfed her. Nothing about him had changed. He was still as perfect as she remembered.

His hair was freshly cut and slicked to the back. He wore a Paper Denim short-sleeve button-up with small planes all over it, black, fitted jeans and grey, YSL Chelsea boots. He matched her fly to a T. There was no way he couldn't see they were meant to be.

"HI," she spoke softly.

"What's up?" Carlos eyed her luscious thighs then pulled off.

Chyna didn't know where they were heading but was thankful just to be near him. He didn't utter a word to her the entire ride but that was ok. The fact that he wanted to see her had to be a good sign. Fifteen minutes later, they parked in front of his house. The fact that he'd taken her back to his spot was an even better sign.

After the way she'd acted, she thought she'd never be invited back again. Carlos unlocked the doors and stepped out. The sun was starting to set. A pink hue cascaded over the sky. It was the perfect day to take a walk and enjoy the good weather but Carlos had some heavy shit that needed to be handled.

Cutting things off with Chyna was probably one of the hardest things in life he'd ever have to do. He wanted to show her the respect she deserved and do it in person and not over the phone. She meant too much to him to do her like that. He hated that she seemed optimistic about them picking up where they left off. She had no idea that this was where their love story would end.

After spending some time with Bellamy, they decided to give their relationship another try. If it hadn't been for the death of their son, they'd still be together. They owed it to each other to see if things could be salvaged. Chyna was sure to flip when he told her the news. She would have every right to be upset but Carlos had tried to do a good job of never leading her on.

He and Chyna walked into his place. Carlos flipped on the lights as she placed her bag down. She was finally back home. She'd missed being in his peaceful sanctuary. Needing something to get his mind right, Carlos turned on some music. He didn't know how he was going to find the words he needed to say. If only she'd chosen him when she'd had the chance, then none of this would be a factor.

Stressed out, he rolled a blunt. He needed something potent to calm his nerves. Carlos leaned against the kitchen island and took a pull off the cigar. Chyna watched without saying a word. She could see he was deep in thought. Hell, she had a lot on her mind too. She loved the fuck outta him and it was time he knew. She'd been a mess without him. Chyna never wanted to feel that type of abandonment again.

With her hands stuffed in the back pocket of her jeans, she sauntered over to him slowly. *Where Did It Go Wrong* by Anthony Hamilton stirred up their emotions.

Boldly, Chyna took the blunt from his hand and placed it up to her ruby red lips. With ease, she blew a cloud of smoke into the air then handed it back to him.

Standing in-between his legs, she wrapped her arms around his waist then rested her head on his firm chest. The sound of his heartbeat soothed her. Carlos knew he should've made her move but it felt good having her near. He knew the longer it took him to tell her where they stood, the deeper the wound would be. But as they stood basking in the essence of one another, the realization came that his feelings for her ran deeper than even he knew.

Carlos wished he could be the man she wanted him to be but he wasn't ready to open his heart to someone new. Chyna looked up at his face. Carlos gazed down into her innocent brown eyes. *This girl is gonna be the death of me,* he thought.

"Will you please forgive me?" Chyna spoke just above a whisper. "I know I fucked up, and sometimes I can be a handful, but I really care about you... I love you," she admitted, feeling a weight lift off her chest.

"There, I said it. I love you and I don't like it 'cause I'm fucked up… and so are you. But even with all that being said, I can't see myself being with anybody else but you." Chyna's eyes shimmered.

Carlos' heart couldn't take the weight of her words.

"I know it's hard for you to say it but I know you love me too." She caressed his face. "Can't nobody love you like me." She wrapped her arms around his neck and kissed him passionately on the lips.

"Who's better for you than me?" She waited for a rebuttable but didn't get one. "No one," she whispered, sucking his bottom lip. "Can't nobody make you feel the way I do." She unbuttoned his shirt.

Carlos couldn't contain himself. He had to have her. Chyna knew exactly how to satisfy his needs. Their sexual chemistry was always a sure thing. Sex was never their problem. They were great together in bed. It was the other rooms in the house they had problems in. She barely knew him but yet claimed to love him.

He never offered his heart to her or asked to be in a relationship. They'd agreed from the beginning that what they shared would be something light and fun. Now here she was trying to add feelings to the equation. And yes, Carlos had a special place for her in his heart. He loved her. He just wasn't sure if he loved what lie between her legs or what lie in her heart.

"Nobody asked you to get me attached to you. In fact, you tricked me." – Alessia Cara, "I'm Yours"

#23

For hours Chyna and Carlos lay wrapped up in his sheets making love. He couldn't believe he'd allowed himself to get sucked back in. Chyna had spun a web so tight around him it was hard for him to break loose. Carlos had never in his 35 years on earth made love to a woman so strong and good.

His dick didn't want to detach from her. How would he ever be able to fuck her and forget her? The notion was easier said than done. Her flesh, her mind and her soul all belonged to him. Carlos didn't want things to end but they had to. He wasn't going to sell her a dream that they were going to be together. Selfishly, he wanted all of her but was only willing to give a quarter of himself. Chyna was a good girl and he was a good dude. In another space and time they would've been the ideal couple but unfortunate circumstances had gotten in the way.

The short ride to her place felt like it took an eternity. For Chyna, the ride was too short. She never wanted to leave his side. The night they spent together was nothing short of magical. It would be a night she cherished forever. She was happy that things between them were back on track. She finally had her baby back. Now she could function and breathe. Life could resume. She could focus on her book and everything else that was great in her life.

Carlos slowly pulled in front of her building. On the outside he seemed cool, calm and collected but on the inside, he was a fuckin' mess. His heart was pounding out of his chest. What he was about to say would change the course of their friendship forever. Chyna turned and looked at him with a huge smile on her face.

"I had fun last night." She bit into her bottom lip and placed her hand over his. "Can I see you later? Black Spade is spinning at Blank Space tonight. I was thinking we could swing through for a minute. Plus, I wanna tell you about what happened at the wedding. Some crazy shit went down."

"Nah, I don't think that's a good idea," Carlos replied barely able to look her in the eye.

"Why? You got something else planned?"

"I don't know how to say this but…"

Chyna unconsciously stopped breathing. A piercing sound echoed in her ear. She knew exactly where this conversation was headed. Anytime anyone started a sentence with *I don't know how to say this but*, some bad shit was coming behind it.

"I'ma need my key back," Carlos said reluctantly.

"Why?"

"'Cause we need to chill for a minute."

Chyna blinked her eyes and tried her damnedest not to shed a tear.

"What you mean we need to chill for a minute?"

Carlos inhaled deep then exhaled. *Fuck*, he thought gripping the steering wheel so tight his fingertips burned.

"Me and Bellamy… getting back together."

"Y'all doing what?" Chyna said confused.

She hadn't seen this coming, or had she just turned a blind eye?

"I never told you this but... when I met you, Bellamy and I were separated and about to get a divorce," Carlos finally confessed.

Chyna furrowed her brows.

"After you dipped, we started back messing around and she got pregnant. Seven months into the pregnancy she went into premature labor. My son only lived two weeks. Shit was hella fucked up between us after that so we got a divorce. But I still love her so... we're trying to work things out."

Chyna could've sworn she'd been kicked in the stomach with a steel-toe boot. *Is this muthafucka serious,* she thought frozen stiff.

"You were married? Y'all had a baby? You love her?" She said in disbelief. "But what about the fact that I love you? Don't that count for something?" Her eyes filled with tears.

"I care about you a lot." Carlos tried to ease her pain.

"You care about me?" Chyna said with an attitude.

"I never wanted this to happen." Carlos shook his head torn up inside.

"What you mean you never wanted this to happen? If you didn't want this to happen, then maybe you shouldn't have fucked me like I was the air you breathe! Maybe you shouldn't have spent so much fuckin' time with me! Maybe you shouldn't have clung to me the way you did at night!"

"Chyna, I never said we was gon' be together," Carlos reasoned. "This shit wasn't supposed to go past Memorial Day weekend. You're the one that showed up on my doorstep at two o'clock in the morning on some other shit. I was fully prepared to walk away. So you tell me. What happened to the girl that didn't want a relationship and just wanted to have fun? When did things get so serious for you?"

"So I'm the one to blame for this? I'm the one that kept this shit going? I'm the one that gave myself Cartier LOVE bracelets? You ain't have nothing to do with it, Carlos? Really?" She shrugged her shoulders.

"Yeah, I played my part," he admitted.

"Fuck yeah you played a part!" Chyna's sadness morphed into anger. "You may not be my boyfriend but you for damn sure act like it! Yo' mouth say one thing but your actions say another."

Chyna was so mad she couldn't think straight. *This muthafucka got a lot of nerve.*

"I can't believe you gon' fuck me then break up with me," she said bewildered.

"Chyna! You are not my girlfriend!" He swung his arm in the air erratically. "See, this why we need to chill 'cause you got shit misconstrued." Carlos fell back in his seat.

"I ain't got shit misconstrued. I know exactly where we stand! You ain't shit! Plain and simple. But what's fucked up is that you came into my life... and made me think that we could be more than what we actually were!"

"I never said that we was gon' be together!" He yelled, mad as hell.

"No, but your actions did. And I'm sorry to hear about your dead baby but maybe you should've told me about that when we started back fuckin' around! You looked me dead in the eye and said you and Bellamy were done, and like a dummy, I believed you," Chyna fumed.

"Little did I know you were married to the bitch! But tell me this," She turned around in her seat so she could get a better look at him. "Did you fuck her?"

Carlos looked out the window. He refused to answer. Answering that question would only open up another can of worms that he didn't want to deal with.

"Did you fuck her?" Chyna squinted her eyes. "Did you fuck her over the last week, 'cause you for damn sure ain't been fuckin' me!"

"I'm not answering that."

"Oh yes the fuck you are! Did... you... fuck... her?" Chyna demanded to know.

"Gone with that bullshit." Carlos waved her off.

"I'm not gon' ask you again. Did you fuck her?"

Carlos sat silent.

"Did you fuck her?!" Chyna repeated. "Did... you... fuck... her?"

"Yeah, I did! That make you feel better?" Carlos quipped.

As soon as he admitted it, Chyna wished she'd never asked the question. Tears the size of lemon drops landed on her chest.

"So you fucked her then you fucked me? Who does that?!" Chyna eyed him with disgust.

"Meeeeeeeeeeeeee! I'm fucked up!" Carlos shouted so loud the veins in his neck popped out.

"You damn right you are." Chyna wiped her face.

All the air in her lungs had escaped. She felt trapped in her own skin.

"I hate myself," Her lip quivered. "'Cause I knew better but I still fell for your shit. I guess that's 'cause I'm fucked up too, right?" Her chest heaved up-and-down.

"But you know what?" She pointed her finger at him. "You're more fucked up… and that's even way too fucked up for me!" She mushed him in the head.

"Yo, chill. Don't put your hands on me," Carlos caught her hand and tossed it back roughly. "I know I should've told you the truth from the jump but I didn't and I'm sorry for that. What I did was fucked up." He apologized sincerely.

"Sorry my ass," Chyna hissed. "Were you inside of her when I left you that voicemail that night?"

Carlos shot her a look that could kill.

"I'm not going there with you. It's over. It's done. Just leave it at that."

Chyna eyed him with contempt.

"I hate that I ever fuckin' met you." She took his key off her key chain and left it on the dashboard.

"But you know what? It's all good. You see me out in the street, act like you don't fuckin' know me. Act like I'm dead... just like your baby!" She got out and slammed the door so hard the window cracked.

Chyna wanted to make him hurt as much as he'd made her. It worked. It took every fiber of Carlos' being not to jump out the car and whoop her ass. He never understood how a man could ever hit a woman until that very second. He knew Chyna was hurt but after the venom she spewed, he'd never be able to view her the same. He'd cut her off but now they were done for good.

"Li'l daddy all in my face." – Chriss

Zoe, "Twerkin' In My Heels"

#24

Tears slid from the corner of Chyna's eyes as she lay on her back gazing blankly at the ceiling. She thought that running away to Chicago would ease her pain but she felt more suffocated there. She never thought that at the age of 33 she'd be dismissed and left behind for the second time. She'd played a game of Russian roulette with her heart and lost her life.

How could Carlos so easily speak his peace and then leave her in limbo? If he felt like things were moving too fast, he could've set the tempo. She would've let him take the driver's seat and rode shot gun. Things between them could've been so simple and that's what killed her mentally. Did she not meet his standards? She thought they were set in stone. How could she have been so wrong?

This wasn't how things were supposed to be. Within seconds, the love she thought they shared was erased like writing in pencil on a page. She never thought she'd see the day when something that seemed so concrete could so easily be thrown away. But there she lay loving him while he loved her- Bellamy.

"Chyna, get up!" Asia yelled, pulling her off the couch. "You're putting a dent in my damn couch!"

"I'm depressed." Chyna whined sliding onto the floor like Selena.

"No! You stink! Get yo' funky-ass up and take a bath! You smell like falafels and fungus!"

"I don't want to," Chyna groaned.

"I know you ain't come all the way to Chicago to funk up my house?"

"I came up here to get some peace and quiet but you keep on bothering me. You're supposed to be taking care of me in my time of need," Chyna whined like a baby.

"I have been taking care of you. Yo' ass been eating up all my goddamn food and my baby's snacks! You been lounging around and not cleaning up behind yo'self since you got here! You act like I'm yo' goddamn maid." Asia placed her hand on her hips.

"Ok, Mom," Chyna shot sarcastically.

"Fuck you. You can't be walking around not washing yo' ass behind no man. I don't give a damn how good the dick is. It ain't that serious, boo-boo."

"I stink that bad?" Chyna smelled underneath her arm.

The tip of her nose almost fell off she stunk so bad.

"Yes, girl, you do. Aiden even said Tee-Tee stink," Asia laughed.

"I'm sorry, friend." Chyna lay in a heap on the floor. "I'm trying to shake this shit but it's hard. I didn't see this shit coming."

"But didn't you?" Asia sat on the edge of the couch and watched her flounder on the floor like a fish.

"You've been sitting here fuckin' a man for two months without a title and then you're surprised when he reminds you of it? You can't be out here fuckin' and expecting a man to buy the milk when he's had the cow for free."

"You callin' me a cow? I ain't no damn cow." Chyna scrunched up her face.

"You know what the hell I mean." Asia hit her in the head with a throw pillow. "If you're going to date someone, then you must date with a purpose. Did you ever ask Carlos what he was looking for or what he wanted? Or did you just assume that y'all were on the same page?"

Chyna lay stumped. She hadn't taken out the time to open her mouth and ask the necessary questions.

"I didn't, but you have to understand that I wasn't expecting to feel this way. I fought loving him but the shit just kind of snuck up on me. And I thought we were on the same page 'cause he treated me like I was his girlfriend. I mean, what man gives a chick a key to his crib and Cartier LOVE bracelets if they don't want to be with them?"

"Carlos!" Asia stated exasperated. "I mean, don't get me wrong. I don't doubt that he has feelings for you. It's obvious that he does but y'all weren't in a relationship. Y'all were in a situationship, beloved. Y'all was over there fuckin' and suckin' and neither of y'all took the time to truly get to know the other. You can't build a relationship off of bumpin' uglies and pillow talk. You know that, Chyna."

"I know." She sighed knowing her friend was telling the truth.

"I mean, what do you know about him besides the fact that he's fine, successful and got a big dick?" Asia died to know.

"Nothing!" She answered for her. "You ain't even know he was married!"

Chyna contemplated her question and realized that in the two months she'd been dealing with Carlos, she hadn't really learned a thing. It dawned on her that she was the one doing all of the talking and revealing. He never opened himself up to her. Did he not trust her or did he feel she was unworthy of knowing his thoughts, hopes and fears?

Or maybe he didn't like her enough. Hell, it took him to cut her off before he revealed he even had a child that passed. Chyna had told him about India, Tyreik, her career dreams and troubles. He hadn't revealed a thing and she never required him to.

"I can't even front. I know a little bit but not a lot."

"Exactly, so be mad at him but also be mad at yourself. Don't ever get lovesick behind a man that's only offering you dick and a smile," Asia urged.

"And Cartier bracelets," Chyna admired her wrist.

"I'm done talkin' to yo' dumb-ass. You ain't learned shit." Asia stood up.

"Yes I have. I swear! I'm just playing!" Chyna wrapped her arms around Asia's leg so she couldn't walk away.

She totally understood everything Asia had to say. She'd played herself. The player had gotten played and now she was dealing with the ramifications of a broken heart.

"I got an idea." Asia peeled Chyna's hands from her ankle. "How about you get off the floor, go in the bathroom, put some soap and hot water on your puss and get dressed so we can go out? 'Cause, chile, you have driven me to drink."

"Do we have to?" Chyna pouted, not in the mood.

"Yes, we do. I'm tired of seeing you look a hot mess." Asia headed out the room.

"Huuuuuh; ok, but I'm not brushing my teeth," Chyna acted like a brat.

"The devil is a lie!"

"I got enemies... I got enemies... got a lotta enemies... got a lotta people tryna drain me of my energy... tryna take the wave from a nigga," Chyna rapped along like she was Drake.

She was in the zone. The Velvet Lounge in Chicago was the place to be on a Friday night. It was a moody cocktail lounge with velvet details. It was one of Chicago's longest running jazz spots. The décor wasn't much to talk about but it was poppin'. That Friday night was hip hop night. It was packed from wall-to-wall. Bodies were pressed up against one another. Chyna vibed out with a cranberry and vodka in her hand.

She examined the atmosphere. All the chicks in the club looked like a bunch of Kim Kardashian wannabes. All the dudes reminded her of the knockoff versions of Kanye West. Chyna hated that no one tried to be original anymore. She thrived on being a trendsetter. Normally, she tried to kill the game when she stepped out but that night she didn't have the energy to try to be cute.

That night she didn't put any effort into her look. She just wanted to be comfortable. She wore a lightweight camo jacket, a gold chain-link necklace, sleeveless, black tee with **Trill** written across the chest, distressed booty shorts and Tims. Instead of a face full of makeup, she rocked a classic wing liner and a matte red lip.

Dressing up in heels and a tight skirt wasn't the move. She wasn't trying to land a man or have a one-night stand. Chyna normally liked to be the center of attention but she honestly just wanted to be left alone. She would've much rather have been at Asia's crib, burying her face in a bowl of Edy's Double Fudge Brownie ice cream. Being in the club wasn't going to cure what ailed her.

She was hurt and it was going to take her some time to heal. That's if she ever did. The thought of what she and Carlos could've been tormented her. Even though he'd lied to her and led her on, she still wanted him. A part of her held out hope that he'd change his mind and come around. He had to see she was the one he needed to be with.

Sure, he and Bellamy had history, but Chyna saw the way he looked at her. Carlos didn't have the same connection with her as he did with Chyna. He didn't have to admit it. She knew he loved her. It was only a matter of time before he came to his senses. Needing a moment to breathe, she told Asia that she was ready to leave. All of the smoke and loud music was making her head hurt. Plus, some dusty bitch was being way too extra and waving her nasty, old, ratty weave in her face.

If Chyna didn't leave soon she was sure to go to jail. She wanted nothing more than to curl up in bed and be sad in peace. Usually when she left the club she hit Carlos up but Chyna knew better. She would never make a fool out of herself twice. She'd had enough of looking dumb. He didn't want her so that was his loss. She would be a'ight eventually. If she could survive breaking up with Tyreik, Chyna could survive anything.

Chyna edged her way through the crowd. Asia was steps ahead of her. She tried her best to keep up but it was hard to push through without stepping on someone's foot. It was so packed that she was nearly knocked down by some tall-ass dude.

"Damn, nigga! Watch where you going!" Chyna shouted as he caught her in his arms.

"My bad, sweetheart." The guy said sincerely. "Hold up... Chyna, is that you?"

Chyna focused in on the dude's face and realized that she'd almost been trampled over by none other than L.A.

"Hey." She responded standing up straight.

Chyna was surprised to see L.A. in Chicago of all places. Nervously, she smoothed down her hair and prayed to God she was cute.

"What you doing up here?" He rested his hand on her hip.

Chyna inhaled deep and tried to play it cool.

"Visiting my best friend." She replied trying to quiet the heartbeat in her clit.

L.A. was one fine muthafucka. Like SWV sang, he could be her Man Crush Monday everyday. The man was that deal. Butterflies fluttered in the pit of her stomach. Seeing him made her forget about Carlos for a brief second.

"That's what's up. Don't tell me you leaving though. I just got here. You gotta come have a drink with me."

"I'm about to head out. I'm tired."

"I understand," L.A. said disappointed. "I'm surprised my boy let you out of his sight. You know he's stingy with his toys."

"Is that right?" She sucked her teeth.

L.A. had a slick way of being funny.

"Chyna!" Asia called out her name.

Chyna blinked her eyes. She'd completely forgotten about Asia.

"I'ma be in the car!" She placed her hands up to her mouth and yelled.

"Alright! Here I come!" Chyna assured then focused her attention back on L.A. "Me and ya man don't fuck around no more." She revealed to see how he would react.

"Let me guess. He and Bellamy are back together again?"

"Bingo." Chyna pointed her fingers like they were a gun.

"That dude crazy, man," L.A. shook his head then licked his lips. "If you were mine, I would never let you go." He stepped closer.

His chest was now pressed up against hers. He could feel Chyna's nipples harden underneath the fabric of her shirt.

"Too bad I'm not yours," she smirked, liking the attention.

She loved to toy with a man's emotions.

"Let me take you out when I get back to St. Louis," L.A. asked seductively.

"I'm not doing that. You and Carlos are friends."

"We cool but we ain't been friends since the 11th grade," he clarified.

"I'm still not fuckin' wit' you," Chyna insisted. "Besides, you don't wanna go out with me."

"Why not?" L.A. questioned.

"I'ma savage. I will eat you alive," Chyna responded stone-faced.

"Give me your phone." L.A. held out his hand.

Chyna eyed him for a second then reluctantly gave in.

"When you get tired of being faithful to a muthafucka that ain't being faithful to you, get at me." He locked his number in her phone then handed it back to her. "Stay pretty, baby girl." He caressed her cheek.

L.A. wanted to kiss her but thought against it. He would have his time with Chyna. It was only a matter of time before she would be his.

Jesus, be a fence. I'ma fuck him, Chyna thought as he disappeared into the crowd.

"You just kept on playin' games." –

Mila J, "Don't" (Cover)

#25

Life for Chyna had literally gone from rainbows and unicorns to vomit and shit. Since she'd returned home from Chicago, she'd spent all of her time in bed sick. She was sick with the flu. Every time she got on an airplane, she fell ill. Airplanes were a death trap of germs. Nothing was worse than being sick in the summertime. Summer colds made you want to kill yourself. Plus, she'd gotten her period which made matters worse. Needing meds and pads, she slipped on an old, oversized, Biggie t-shirt that belonged to Tyreik, a pair of black leggings with bleach stains on them and Tims.

Chyna's hair was all over her head, so she threw on an OBEY snapback and headed out the door. The cab she ordered was outside her door waiting on her. Chyna looked like a li'l ugly, snotty nose, boy but she didn't care. She looked as miserable as she felt. Her nose was stopped up, her throat itched and she coughed every other minute.

"I'm going to the Walgreens off of Lafayette." She instructed the driver.

The cab driver turned on the meter and they were on their way. Chyna caught a glimpse of her reflection and stifled a scream. She looked terrible. Her skin was a blue-green shade. Her nose was raw from blowing it so much. She had to get some medicine and get better fast. It was the middle of August and she still hadn't written a word. If she didn't come up with a book idea soon, she was fucked. Less than five minutes later the cab driver pulled into the Walgreens' parking lot. It was packed as usual.

"I'll be right back." She told the driver.

The Walgreens' entrance door parted as she strode into the store. In a rush to get what she needed and leave, Chyna bypassed the carts and headed straight to the baby/feminine hygiene aisle. Chyna quickly grabbed a pack of Kotex Overnight pads and then raced over to the medicine aisle. There were so many different types of cold medicines it was hard for her to choose.

Her head had begun to hurt from the decision-making. Chyna needed to get out of there and head home so she could get back in bed. Stooping down, she read the description off the back of a Robitussin box. She needed something that was going to break up the phlegm in her nose and chest. As she read the information, she heard the sound of Carlos' laughter float through the air.

Her heart raced a mile per minute. *It can't be*, she thought shooting to her feet. Chyna stood on her tippy toes to see over the aisle. Sure enough, there he was with a smile on his face so bright it eclipsed the sun. To make matters worse, he wasn't alone. Bellamy was right by his side. Chyna crumbled and turned to dust as she watched another woman make the man she loved laugh.

"Fuck. What am I going to do?" She said underneath her breath.

She couldn't let them see her this way. Carlos would think she looked a mess because of him. Outside of her being sick, it was partially true. He still hadn't escaped the deepest parts of her brain. Whenever she closed her eyes, there he was. He'd taken control of her dreams. The taste of him still lingered on her tongue.

Chyna looked down at the pack of pads in her hand and panicked. Shook, she threw them to the side as Carlos and Bellamy turned into the aisle. She tried to play it off as if she hadn't seen them coming but the pack of pads landed at Bellamy's feet with a thud. Chyna quickly turned her back to them and prayed they'd walk past without noticing her.

"I think you dropped these, ma'am." Bellamy tapped her on the shoulder, unaware of who she was.

"Me no speak no Inglés." Chyna replied with her head down and her hat cocked low.

"Chyna?" Carlos placed his hand on her shoulder and turned her around.

Fuck. Chyna rolled her eyes and faced them.

"Oh, hi." She shot him a fake smile.

"Ooooh, you look terrible," Bellamy looked at her like she stank.

"I'll take those." Chyna snatched the pads from her hand.

"You can have them, honey. Heavy flow?" Bellamy giggled at the fact that she had a pack of long, thick, overnight maxi pads.

Chyna wanted to shrivel up and die. *Really, God? This how you do yo' girl,* she thought tucking the pads under her arm. She stood there looking like a homeless person while Bellamy resembled an Instagram model. Her long hair cascaded down her back into an abundance of curls. She rocked a brown, silk, billowing tank that was tucked inside of a pair of white, wide-leg trousers and a tan Hermès Birkin bag. Chyna understood why Carlos was in love with the bitch. She was stunning. At that moment, she put Chyna to shame.

"You good?" Carlos asked genuinely concerned.

He wanted to be a dick to her but his anger fell short. Chyna usually was put together but that day she looked like she was down to her last dollar. Her face was pale and ashen. Dried tears graced the corners of her eyes. A knife went through his heart because he knew he was the cause of her misery.

"I have the flu." Chyna looked anywhere but his eyes.

She refused to look at him. If she did she was sure to cry. Having him that close and not being able to reach out and touch him was cruel and unusual punishment.

"I hope you feel better." Carlos tried to make eye contact with her but she wouldn't give in.

His natural reaction whenever he was around her was to comfort and take care of her. But all of that was over now. Her final words to him were still fresh in his mind. He felt bad that she wasn't feeling well but he'd never be able to forgive her.

"Babe, you ready?" Bellamy linked arms with him, feeling insecure.

She could see the yearning in his eyes when he looked at Chyna and didn't like it one bit.

"Yeah." He replied walking past Chyna.

Now that they were gone, Chyna licked her lips and tried not to cry. There was no way she was going to embarrass herself in the middle of Walgreens. She was already humiliated enough. The meter was running. She had to get out of there. Seeing Carlos with Bellamy verified that they were done for good. She had to move on with her life and forget all about him. She was too fly to be stressing over a dude that didn't want her.

He didn't owe her anything and neither did she. If he could say fuck her and flaunt his ex-wife in her face as if it were nothing, then two could play that game. As soon as Chyna was back to 100 percent, she would take L.A. up on his offer for a date.

"Fuck Carlos." She spat heading towards the checkout lane.

"Had more than enough time to make up... It's easy to see I was fed up. But now I'm on a whole 'nother level. Look, he only took your place 'cause you let him," Chyna sang at the top of her lungs.

She was putting the finishing touches on her outfit. L.A. would be there at any minute. Chyna felt a little weary about what she was about to do but her heart was on fuck it mode. She didn't want to feel anything for anyone. Her happiness was all that mattered. She'd been sad and shut-in long enough.

Carlos wasn't in his feelings about her. He'd gone on with life. Now it was time she did the same. It was fucked up that she'd be moving on with his pot'nah but the saying was true: hurt people, hurt people. Summer was winding down and Chyna was going to enjoy every minute she had left. Fuck sitting in the house crying over a muthafucka that wasn't checkin' for her.

She had to remind herself that she was the shit. She didn't sweat muthafuckas. They sweat her. But as she took one last look at herself in the mirror, she couldn't help but wish she was getting pretty to go out with Carlos instead. Chyna could play hard all day. She could act like she was good and that she didn't care, but the truth lied in her heart. Nothing or no one would be able to compare to Carlos.

Plain and simple, he did it for her. He'd become her moral compass. He made her want to be a better person. With him she was centered. Now that he was gone, she'd reverted back to her reckless ways. Caring never got her anywhere. This was why she guarded her heart at any cost. She never wanted to fall in love with Carlos but she took a leap of faith and tried her hand at opening up and failed.

It was ok though, 'cause the way she was looking had her feeling like she was the baddest bitch on the planet. She'd grown her hair out at the top. Her natural curls spiraled on the top of her head. She rocked a deep, side-part just like Basketball Wives star Laura Govan. Her face was painted and dusted to the gods.

She rocked a strong brow, KoKo lashes and a matte berry-colored lip. Her Christian Dior, black, square shades was the only accessory she wore besides the Cartier LOVE bracelets Carlos had given her. She couldn't get the damn things off because she didn't have the screw. He did. It wasn't like she'd really tried hard to. She could've easily gone to the Cartier store and had them removed. Chyna secretly enjoyed rocking a reminder of the time they'd spent together.

The rest of her look consisted of a black, sleeveless bodysuit, grey skinny jeans with a hole ripped at each of the knees and black, leather, pointed-toe Gianvito Rossi heels. Chyna was back to her old sex kitten ways and loving it.

"These hoes better watch they man!" She gagged as L.A. texted her to let her know he was at the door.

Chyna grabbed her Saint Laurent monogram, metallic, tassel clutch and headed downstairs. She didn't know where they were going but her outfit was chic enough for all occasions. Chyna opened the door and her clit set on fire. She almost had to fan her pussy so she wouldn't take him upstairs and sit on his dick.

She and L.A. would have some great one-on-one fun. Homeboy could get it on sight. His butterscotch skin matched hers while his thick brows and neatly trimmed beard sucked her in. L.A. was a tall drink of water. She wanted to devour every last drop of him. He wore an oxblood-colored, cashmere t-shirt, maroon, fitted, skinny jeans, a pair of Maroon 6's and a gold Rolex watch. A gold, ruby ring gleamed from his pinky finger.

"What's up, beautiful?" He grinned, kissing her on the cheek.

And he's wearing Clive Christian cologne, she salivated. Clive Christian cologne cost $900 a bottle and it smelled like money. *I am not gon' fuck him. I am not gon' fuck him,* Chyna chanted over and over again in her mind.

"Hi." She kept a straight face.

She wasn't going to let L.A. know she was feeling him.

"You ready?" He asked.

"Yeah. Where we going?" She asked locking the door.

"It's a surprise."

"You and yo' homeboy wit' y'all surprises," Chyna said so low only she could hear.

"Huh? What you say?" L.A. asked opening the passenger side door.

"Nothing," she giggled getting inside.

The car ride to their destination ended up being almost thirty minutes. Chyna had started to fall asleep. To her dismay, they pulled up in front of The Ambassador. The Ambassador was one of St. Louis' oldest concert venues. It was located in the heart of North St. Louis. Chyna hadn't been there in six years. She didn't venture out to the county too much. North County was way too hood and filled with racist cops.

"What's going on here tonight?" She looked at him sideways.

"Corey Holcomb performing." L.A. parked his car.

Chyna sneered. She loved Corey Holcomb. He was one of her favorite comedians. She just didn't want to see him at The Ambassador.

"What's wrong? You don't want to go in?"

"I just wish I would've known we were coming here. I would've worn another outfit," she frowned.

Her outfit was way too cute for The Ambassador. The Ambassador was the type of place you wore Tims or

J's to. A fight or shootout could break out at any moment and a bitch had to be prepared to run for cover.

"You look fine, c'mon." L.A. got out.

"The first time I hear a gunshot, we up out this bitch." Chyna switched her hips.

L.A. couldn't take his eyes off her ass. Chyna had the perfect, small, round butt. He truly loved her outer appearance but wanted to get to know what she had going on upstairs. Nothing turned him off more than a dumb-ass woman. At first his intentions were to get on her to one-up Carlos but L.A. found himself really digging Chyna.

He was at a point in his life where he was tired of playing around. He'd had all the quote, unquote bad bitches. He was looking for a woman of substance; someone he could share his life with. Being rich and successful with no one to share it with was a pitiful thing. He wasn't getting any younger. He wanted marriage and kids. If Chyna played her cards right, she could very well be the future Mrs. Lucas Abbot.

L.A. had gotten them seats in the VIP section of the comedy show. As they navigated their way through the table and chairs, Chyna spotted Carlos in the distance. He was sitting in the same section with his homeboy, Fab, and Bellamy. A cold sweat washed over her as he spotted her.

Carlos honestly couldn't believe his eyes. His eyes had to be playing tricks on him. There was no way in hell that Chyna was at The Ambassador with L.A. of all people. She would never stoop that low, or so he thought. Yeah, he'd done her wrong and cut her off, but she didn't have to get him back like that. She cut him deep with this shit.

He never saw this betrayal coming. At first Chyna thought going out with L.A. would be a good idea. That was until she saw the look on Carlos' face. Anger radiated off his skin. She'd pushed him past his breaking point. Spotting the crew, L.A. stopped at their table to speak.

"What up, fam?" He gave Fab and Carlos a pound. "How you doing, Bellamy?" He leaned over and gave her a hug.

"Hi, baby." She air-kissed his cheek.

Carlos eyed Chyna with venom in his eyes. He was so mad he thought he was going to combust. Carlos gazed over at her wrist and noticed that she was still wearing the Cartier bracelets. The fact that she was still rocking them let him know she still cared.

"You a wild boy," Fab chuckled at the fact that he was there with Chyna.

"Stop it. Ain't nobody trippin'. We all grown. Ain't that right, Los?" L.A. smirked wrapping his arm around Chyna's neck and pulling her close.

Chyna was heated. She'd begun to think that L.A. had brought her there to be funny. *This nigga knew he was gon' be here*, she fumed. He was using her in his battle to see whose dick was bigger again and she'd fallen for it. Chyna wanted to slap the black off of him, but she had to remind herself that she was using him too.

"It's all good, fam. I'm happy with mines." Carlos turned Bellamy's face towards his and kissed her on the lips.

He knew the sight would kill Chyna. He hoped she died a slow death. Chyna chuckled and shook her head. Carlos had just pulled the ultimate sucka move. She was tired of the back and forth game they'd been playing with one another. He'd done her dirty and now she'd gotten her revenge. They were even. She was done. She'd played this game years ago with Tyreik and Dame and lost. She wasn't about to play herself again and come out on the bottom.

"Take me home." She snapped before walking towards the door.

L.A. ran behind her.

"Ay yo! Wait up!" He jogged. "Slow down!" He finally caught up to her.

"Did you know he was going to be here?" Chyna spun around on her heels.

L.A. stopped abruptly in his tracks.

"On my mama, I didn't know," he replied truthfully.

Chyna eyed him suspiciously. She believed him but was still pissed.

"What's the problem though? It's a wrap between y'all, right? Unless you still got feelings for him."

Chyna exhaled her frustrations and didn't respond.

"You over him or nah? 'Cause I'm really diggin' you and I wanna get to know you better. But if you still got feelings for ole boy, then I'ma fall back." L.A. held up his hands.

He was nobody's second choice. He wanted Chyna all to himself. He wanted her to dig him as much as he dug her.

"I ain't never fuckin' wit' Carlos again," Chyna stated with such confidence that even she believed her own lies.

"I stood all the jealousy, all the bitchin'
too. Yes, I'd forget it all once in bed
with you." – Marvin Gaye, "Just To
Keep You Satisfied"

#26

Thunder clashed amongst the midnight sky. It was pouring rain outside. Thick rain drops tapped against Chyna's window pane. She was happy that she'd made it home when she did and hadn't stayed at the comedy show. It was raining so hard the trees outside her window swayed in the wind. She sat on the edge of her bed dressed in her panties and bra.

Seeing Carlos again with Bellamy had really fucked her up. She had to figure out a way to get him out of her system. She'd lied and told L.A. that they were done but she didn't know if that was entirely true. She still had a lot of pain that she hadn't dealt with. He still ran through her mind all day long, although he shouldn't be.

He had a hold or some kind of control over her that needed to be broken. She couldn't continue to live like this but her heart wouldn't let her fallback. Going and messing with another dude didn't help at all. He'd embedded himself in her veins. All Chyna wanted was him.

"Lord, I don't wanna love him no more," she cried.

Chyna's tears scorched her face. She needed help. Being at home alone only made things worse. All she had was her tears and the rain outside as comfort. Carlos had to know that she missed him with all of her heart. He'd made an impact on her life. She had to have made a big impression on him too. Little did Chyna know, but she'd made an huge impact on him.

She'd affected him in such a way that he wasn't able to finish out his night. She'd completely ruined it with her stunt. He didn't expect much from L.A., but he did from her. At one point she was his baby. That didn't go away overnight. Seeing her with L.A. made him realize how much it hurt her to see him with Bellamy. The game they were playing had to end but Carlos had a few more things to say to her before he said his final goodbye.

Chyna had completely forgotten about the key she'd given him until she heard the sound of heavy footsteps come up her steps. Her heart nearly jumped out of her chest as he reached the top. He was soaking wet from the rain. His white t-shirt clung to his pecks. Carlos looked around to see if she was alone. If L.A. was there, there was sure to be a murder. He was pleased to see that she was there by herself.

Pain and regret was written all over her face. Chyna didn't even try to hide her tears. He needed to see the affect he had on her. Carlos walked over. He had every intention on cussing her out but all of his anger disappeared. Without saying a word, he caressed the side of her face. Chyna trembled under his touch as he lay on top of her. She cried even harder as he ravished her lips with his tongue.

Carlos had no business being there. Although he'd come to tell her off, this was what he secretly yearned for. The entire world vanished when he was with her. Nothing else mattered but him and her. Chyna was his baby and would always be. He hated that they'd ended up like this. He wanted to hold her in his arms forever but forever wasn't in the cards for them. Too much had transpired for them to ever be together.

"I never loved nobody the way I love you," Chyna whimpered as he stroked her middle.

She knew it was too late for them but still held out hope that they could rekindle their romance. Carlos hated to see her cry. All he could do to ease her discomfort was show her how much he hurt too. A single tear fell from his eye. What he couldn't say with his mouth, he revealed through his emotions. He loved her deeply.

He never wanted to let go. Money, sex, weed or Bellamy couldn't get him as high as this. Chyna made him levitate. She was his drug of choice. As a man, he'd done things that he was ashamed of when it came to her. He'd forever regret making her cry. Chyna had been through enough. Every tear she cried hurt him to the core. Carlos wished he could love her the way she wanted but his heart wouldn't allow it. It was still too raw from the loss of his son and everything else he'd gone through.

Carlos had deep baggage that needed to be sorted out. It was fucked up but he loved two women. He didn't want to mistreat either of them. He knew he couldn't keep toying with Chyna's emotions. Jumping in and out of her life was a no-no but damn she felt good. Carlos held her chin in his hand and stared deep in her eyes. He wanted to love her and leave her but the fact still remained that their hearts had become one.

"You're mine," he whispered.

"Mom!" India called out placing her luggage down.

Chyna jumped out of her sleep wondering if she was hearing things. India wasn't supposed to be home for another week.

"Mom! You sleep? I'm home!" India raced up the steps.

"India!" Chyna hopped out of the bed and placed on a robe.

She looked over at Carlos who was still sound asleep. Chyna quietly slipped out of the room to greet her baby girl. She met India on the second floor. Her daughter was the spitting image of her. India looked just like Chyna at the age of fifteen. She had wild, curly hair and skin the color of the sun. Tears of joy flooded Chyna's eyes. Her baby girl, her rib was home.

"What are you doing home early?" She squeezed her tight.

"I couldn't wait another day. I was ready to come home. Europe was fun but there is nothing like home. I missed my mom." India relished being in her mother's arms.

She'd dreamt of this moment the entire plane ride home.

"I missed mama's baby." Chyna placed a sea of kisses all over her face.

Having India home was like a dream come true. Chyna already felt ten times better. India was the ultimate mood booster.

"Did I wake you? Where you asleep?" India stepped back and looked at her mother.

"Umm," Chyna pulled her robe together.

She was naked underneath.

"Yeah, I was umm…" Chyna blushed nervously.

"You got company?" India curled her upper lip.

The thought of her mother being with a man made her sick to her stomach.

"Mama gotta have a life too," Chyna laughed.

"Ewww, Mom!" India covered her face, disgusted. "I'm going downstairs." She turned to leave.

"I love you!" Chyna yelled behind her. "Get dressed and put on some clothes! We'll go get something to eat!"

"Ok!" India skipped down the steps.

Chyna sighed and headed back to her bedroom. In the light of day, all of the night's burdens re-emerged. Things between her and Carlos were more complicated than ever. Now that her daughter was home, she didn't have time to be stuck in limbo. Carlos was going to have to shit or get off the pot. Chyna walked into her bedroom and closed the door behind her.

Carlos was up and putting on his clothes. He glanced over at Chyna out of the corner of his eye. An awkward silence swept over the room. Neither of them knew what to say. Carlos stood up and put on his jeans.

"So your daughter's home?" He finally said.

"Yeah." Chyna answered on edge.

"That's good. I know you're happy." He placed on his shoes.

"I am." Chyna leaned her back against the door.

Small talk was not Carlos' thing. He had to get out of there.

"Well, let me get out of here so y'all can spend some time together." He said fully clothed.

Chyna held onto the doorknob tight. She wasn't going to let him out the door until she got some answers. Carlos stood in front of her.

"You gon' let me by?" He laughed.

Chyna cocked her head to the side. She had to be strong and stand her ground.

"So what now?" She asked with a serious expression on her face.

"C'mon, man," Carlos groaned. "We're in the same place we were before. Ain't nothing changed. You know that, or did you forget that you were on a date with my homeboy last night?"

Chyna hung her head and bit into her bottom lip. He'd done it to her again. *I'm so fuckin' stupid*, she thought. *I am done with this shit.*

"Ok." She picked her head back up.

If he thought she was going to breakdown and cry and beg him to be with her, he had another thing coming. She was getting off this fucked up merry-go-round. Carlos wasn't going to treat her like an afterthought or an easy lay. She was worth more than that. Chyna placed her shoulders back and opened the door. It was time for him to go.

Carlos was slightly surprised that she didn't put up a fight. He was expecting her to get mad but Chyna was as cool as a cucumber. Caught off guard by her response, he stepped out of the room. Chyna followed him down the steps to the front door. Once they got there, Carlos turned to her and said, "Talk to you later."

"No, you won't," she replied confidently.

Carlos looked at her to see if she was serious. She was. He could tell by the unwavering look in her eye; she was done messing with him for good.

"A'ight." He shrugged his shoulders and headed to his car.

Chyna inhaled deep and locked the door. A smile crept into the corner of her lips. She never felt stronger. She was truly proud of herself.

"Mom, who was that?" India poked her head out of her room and asked.

Chyna looked over at her. India had no idea the kind of effect the man who left had on her mother and never would.

"Nobody."

TO BE CONTINUED

CPSIA information can be obtained at www.ICGtesting.com
Printed in the USA
LVOW10s1828310516

490611LV00017B/1152/P